LAST STOP LIBERTY

Into the peaceful town of Liberty comes Bart Honer, the new bank manager, and he is quick to see how fragile the small farmers' finances really are. Setting out to destroy every one of them, he hires King, who he thinks is a no-good drifter, to burn down the barn belonging to Hank and Jessie Meadows. The town sheriff seems to be getting nowhere fast, so Hank takes the law into his own hands . . .

D D LANG

LAST STOP LIBERTY

Complete and Unabridged

LINFORD
Leicester

First published in Great Britain in 1996 by
Robert Hale Limited
London

First Linford Edition
published 1997
by arrangement with
Robert Hale Limited
London

British Library CIP Data

Lang, D D
    Last stop Liberty.—Large print ed.—
Linford western library
    1. Western stories
    2. Large type books
    I. Title
    823.9′14 [F]

ISBN 0–7089–5134–1

Published by
F. A. Thorpe (Publishing) Ltd.
Anstey, Leicestershire

Set by Words & Graphics Ltd.
Anstey, Leicestershire
Printed and bound in Great Britain by
T. J. International Ltd., Padstow, Cornwall

This book is printed on acid-free paper

To Ed, who sits quietly
and lets it all happen

1

UNDER cover of darkness, the masked man struck a match and set aflame the wadding tied round the arrow. He had to be quick. Grabbing the bow, he placed the arrow over his left hand and pulled back to the string — taut — careful not to let the flaming end burn his hand.

He sighted the barn and raised the bow a tad and allowed for the cool night breeze and then he let loose.

He readied another arrow, but he didn't light this one — yet. The man stood and watched as the flaming arrow arced through the night sky and embedded itself in the roof of the barn he'd aimed at.

He waited.

The small flame, barely visible, began to grow as the breeze fanned the tiny orange glow.

As he watched, the roof of the barn exploded in a sheet of flame that he hadn't thought possible. They must've put pitch on the roof, he guessed.

Even against the black sky, he could make out the thick, blacker smoke, rising up towards the stars on this moonless night.

He replaced the second arrow in his quiver and mounted his saddleless pinto, a horse he'd picked because it had no shoes, and rode off into the inky blackness of the prairie.

At a safer distance, the rider stopped and looked back over his shoulder. A thermal rose into the air carrying with it burning embers that gradually faded, then the roof collapsed and a boiling mass of flame and sparks shot even higher into the air.

The man smiled, dug his heels into the flanks of the pony, and rode on without ever looking back again.

★ ★ ★

Jessie Meadows turned in her sleep. She tossed and turned as the buffaloes charged towards her and there was no escape from their thunderous hoofs. She parted her lips to scream as the dust sent up by the charging herd filled her mouth and — she woke up.

The eerie light that filled the curtained-off corner of the small house built slap-bang in the middle of two-thousand acres of rich farmland and prairie, shouldn't be there. It took her a few moments to realize that all was not well.

"Hank! Hank! Wake up, darn it. Something's on fire!"

Her husband, roused from a deep sleep, jumped out of bed and donned his jeans before he even knew what he was doing.

Jessie ran across the room to the window just as the roof of the barn caved in.

"Oh my Lord," she wails, clasping her hands to her face. "The barn's ablaze!"

3

Her husband, wiping the sleep from his eyes is instantly awake.

Grabbing his boots, he headed towards the blazing barn that stored their present — and their future.

"Jess, get to the well!" he yelled as he took a wooden bucket from outside the wood shed and got as close to the barn as the flames would allow before throwing its contents as hard as he can.

It makes no difference whatsoever.

The barn is lost. Worse than that, the seed for the spring are lost with them. The seed that the bank in Liberty owned, lock, stock and barrel. Gone.

Even the plaintive whinnying of their two mares is lost on Hank as he sinks down to the ground on his haunches and watches helplessly as his life goes up in flames.

Jessie stands by his side. She placed one hand on his shoulder and the pair, silhouetted in the flames, just watch.

The horses grow silent as the flames do their work and almost as quickly as it had started, the tinder-dry wood is spent and, as the walls cave in, there is little evidence left to show that a barn, containing, seed, feed, ploughs, hay and animals, ever existed.

Hank hung his head, tears, whether from the heat or sorrow, ran down his soot blackened cheeks, leaving small, white rivers in their wake.

"That's it, Jess. I guess they won."

"No they ain't," his wife snapped, "an' I don't want to hear no defeatist talk like that from you. We bin in worse positions. We'll manage."

Hank stood up and looked at his wife. How come, he thought, women, the weaker sex, are so dang strong? He took her in his arms and held her tight. He wasn't sure if it was for his benefit, hers or maybe for the both of them.

They held each other as the flames began to die down. One side of them as warm as can be, the other side cold as the breeze swept across the prairie.

"You're right, darlin'," Hank said. "You're right."

Together, they turned their back on the once-was barn and returned to the house.

Jessie stoked up the wood-burner and filled the coffee pot. In less time than it took Hank to clean up, a steaming mug of coffee was waiting on him and, next to that, a whiskey bottle and two glasses.

"Whiskey? At four in the mornin'?" Hank said incredulously.

"We got ourselves a mite of work to get through today," Jessie smiled up at him. "This'll be the last time we warm our bones until we're set right."

She poured out two small shots and tipped hers into the coffee.

"Here's to us," she said and took a small sip of the hot, laced, coffee.

"To us," said Hank and downed his tumbler. It didn't taste all that bad, he thought.

"Sun'll be up soon," Jessie said. "We'll see what can be salvaged — if anythin'."

"Won't be much there," Hank said.

"Might be able to save the ploughs, maybe make a new harness, fix some outriggers on the plough and drag it behind me, if'n I have to."

"That's more like the Hank Meadows I married," Jessie said and took another sip of the coffee.

In truth, it tasted awful to her, but it *had* done the trick.

"I'll fry up some eggs and ham an' then let's git to it," she said.

Their collective mood had done a double-take change, as she knew it would. Hank was now positive and eager to get going.

Breakfast over, he donned his overalls, grabbed his hat and rooted through the chest of drawers for the thick leather gloves he kept for winter.

The sun had just popped up over the distant horizon and, behind the house, out in the chicken coop, the old cockerel began his bellyaching. Things sounded normal anyway, Hank thought.

The barn was by now a heap of

smouldering embers, Hank could feel the heat on his face as he stood where the double-hanging doors used to be.

Kicking at the soot Hank found one of the hinges and the bracket still connected. Good, he thought, they'll come in handy when I rebuild the barn.

Hank went through the smouldering pile with a fine tooth comb. Every now and then, flames began licking up as he let the air get at some piece of wood that had miraculously escaped the inferno of the night before.

Soon, a small pile of metal objects took shape on the ground between the barn and house: a hoe, ploughblade, some horseshoes, a rake, three or four bits, one with some leather still attached, a milk urn that looked the worse for wear and of course, the four hinges from the door.

Jessie, having cleaned up inside, now came out to lend a hand.

"Flames sure helped the chickens lay," she said. "We got four more'n we normally get."

"Bright side to everything, I guess," Hank said, and they both laughed.

Hank and Jessie Meadows had been married twelve years. Hank had arrived in Liberty a strapping twenty-four-year old with a shock of blond hair that matched Jessie's almost to a tee.

Six-foot tall in his stockinged feet, Jessie had fallen hopelessly in love with him as soon as he stepped down from the old Wells Fargo stage.

She was sixteen and never been kissed — never even wanted to be — until she saw Hank.

He'd been flattered, of course. Jessie had appeared everywhere Hank was, in the store, where he started working, down by the creek when he went fishing. In less than three months, they were married and had never looked back since.

They'd tried for children, of course, but the good Lord hadn't seen fit to bestow any yet, and deep down, Jessie doubted he ever would.

They'd both worked hard, saving as much as they could until, four years ago, they'd bought this spread. They hadn't given it a fancy name: it was just the Meadows' place, and that's how they liked it.

The first two years had been hard. Borrowing money from the bank to set up, mortgaging the place twice more in the interim, the third year had seen enough return to pay back most, but not all, of what they owed. The fourth year paid back the rest, but with nothing to spare, so the bank kept hold of the deeds and advanced them money for this year's crop.

Now, he guessed he'd have to go, cap in hand to the bank, and borrow some more money. Well, Hank dismissed those thoughts from his mind. If it took another four or five years, then so be it.

Hank took his wife in his soot-stained arms and hugged her like there'd be no tomorrow.

"You git it done?"

"Sure did, went up like a box o' Chinese crackers."

"Good."

The short, fat, besuited man lifted his spectacles higher up his nose and locked his fingers together in front of him, as a smile crossed his greasy-looking face.

Bart Honer, bank manager and would-be land-grabber, was in his element.

Arriving in Liberty to replace Coln Diller, the previous manager, shot up in a bank robbery, he saw the potential for fulfilling his frustrated dreams of being a wealthy man — albeit at the expense of others.

The Meadows' place seemed like a good place to start. Two miles north of town, it boasted some of the richest pasture land around and, although the little house would have to be demolished in order to build a house more in keeping with Honer's expectation of his position, he'd set his sights on starting his empire building there.

Handing over fifty dollars — much more than he wanted to pay, but it was the bank's money — he told the man sitting opposite his desk that he'd be in touch.

Dirk King took the money and stuffed it in his shirt pocket.

"Aren't you going to count it?" Bart asked.

"If'n it ain't all there, I'll be back," Dirk replied.

The look in the tall man's eyes sent a shiver down Honer's back. There was no way he'd cheat on this man — not yet, anyways.

Dirk King was thirty-five, tall, black-haired with a stubble on his chin that didn't seem to grow, it was just — there. His piercing brown eyes had been a lady-killer in his late teens and twenties, but his gun was the love of his life now.

A loner, he'd travelled in more places than most people dreamed of. Never settling, he took whatever work was offered. He had no conscience, he'd do *anything* for the right price.

Honer had met him in the Gold Nugget saloon on the third day after arriving in Liberty. There was something about the man — maybe his twin-Colts worn low and the fact he dressed entirely in black, except for a white bandanna tied round his neck.

The man was mean, of that Honer was certain and, as he'd spent the first three days of his new job familiarizing himself with the accounts held at the bank, he had a fair idea of the vulnerable clients. The Meadows were it.

He'd had a hard job getting the man to have a drink with him, let alone talk, but eventually, money did the talking and Bart Honer had himself a gunman.

Bart Honer was in his late forties, fat, greasy and a lousy manager. The

Union Bank had been looking for some remote place to send him for some time, and Liberty seemed ideal.

Honer knew he'd reached as high as he was going to get and that had turned him into a bitter, twisted man.

Never married, never had a girl come to that, he'd saved more than he spent, but he had no one to spend it on.

At first he'd fought about the transfer. He didn't want to leave Flagstaff: he'd been born there and, although he had no friends, plenty of people knew him. Little did he know that those same people breathed a sigh of relief as he left.

The journey to Liberty had taken a little over four days. Four days of bumpy trails, dust, the threat of Indian attacks which never materialized, lumpy, uncomfortable beds and travelling companions in the stagecoach who'd sized him up after ten minutes and then rarely spoke unless spoken to, which was not often.

He'd entered the small bank as if

a fanfare of bugles should greet him; they hadn't. The staff — two women — hardly looked up as he entered, and when they did, they wished they hadn't bothered.

The job had a small house, as befitting a bank manager in a small town and Honer took the ledgers there every night, poring over the columns of figures so that by the end of that third day, he knew exactly what he was going to do and to whom.

He'd drawn up a list of names, the amount they owed the bank, the size of their places and their locations.

This list he kept in a tin box and placed it under lock and key underneath the brass-framed bed that all but filled his small, lonely bedroom.

But, he thought, it wouldn't be small and lonely for long. With money and power, he could buy whatever and whoever he wanted. And that's just exactly what he intended to do.

Better a big fish in a small pond, he mused.

He watched the gunman leave, wishing he could portray the same vision as Dirk King. Not an ounce of flesh on the man, good looking, in a swarthy, rough sort of way. The complete physical opposite of Honer.

He didn't dwell on that too long though. Pretty soon, he'd be *the* man in town. Someone the whole town would respect — and fear.

He didn't know what he wanted most — their respect or their fear. He'd settle for either.

2

IT didn't take long for word to spread — not only through Liberty but also through the surrounding country — that the Meadows' place had been hit.

Descriptions were, of course, varied: ranging from an Indian attack and massacre, to Hank accidentally dropping an oil-lamp in the barn, and there were many variances in between; one thing a small community loved, and that was gossip.

Pretty soon, at least as soon as their own chores were completed, neighbours rallied round Hank and Jessie Meadows, giving advice — freely — as well as promises of help to raise a new barn.

The barn was a priority. No point in bringing in the harvest if there was no place for it to go.

Trees were hewn over the next week and lumber prepared; building a barn was a cause for celebration at each step of its construction and the beer and whiskey flowed as soon as each stage was completed.

Hank had saved the iron hinges and brackets as well as a few feed troughs, several hoes and rakes and each were reused. No sense in wasting good materials. Besides, they cost money to replace — money they just didn't have.

Harness and tackle arrived, compliments of various neighbours and a horse was supplied on permanent loan. The rakes and hoes had new wooden handles fashioned and the Liberty blacksmith honed the plough and built a new frame.

In ten days, the barn had been completely rebuilt, the ashes of the old one spread over the fields like an act of burial.

The day it was finished meant a barn dance that night. Hay was brought in to serve as chairs and tables, they had two fiddle players and a banjo as well as a tub-thumper.

Food was supplied by everyone who came as well as beer and the biggest bowl of punch you ever did see.

Suddenly, from the depths of depression, Hank and Jessie realized how lucky they were to have good neighbours and knew their neighbours were their friends.

The hoe-down was a great success with everyone — except Bart Honer.

He sat alone in one corner of the new barn clutching a mug of punch and inside he was seething.

Honer was not used to such community spirit, especially from folks who were barely scratching a living from the soil themselves. So their generosity towards one of their own was a complete mystery to him — and totally unexpected.

What Honer had expected was a contrite Hank Meadows coming into the bank, cap in hand, begging for money or credit that Honer *could* give but wouldn't.

A simple foreclosure on the bank's behalf and then he'd purchase the land at a price he'd determine and under a false name. Perfect.

Now, he'd have to revise his plan. The anger he felt towards this small group of poor sodbusters was intense. He sat gripping the tin mug so hard his knuckles were white and he wore a fixed grin on his face, to all the world as happy as they.

Let's see how quick they rally round when *this* barn is razed to the ground, he thought. That thought made him smile and Jessie caught his eye. A fine looking woman, maybe it would be a good idea to get rid of Hank Meadows, too. Might cost him more than fifty bucks, but, with the land and Jessie as a reward, it might just be worth it. Yes-siree!

"You havin' a good time, Mr Honer?" Jessie asked as she approached.

"Fine ma'am," Honer replied. "An'

I thank you kindly for the invite."

"You're welcome, Mr Honer. Care to dance?"

"I haven't danced in years an' I doubt I could, now," Honer replied, a sweat breaking out on his greasy upper lip.

"Come on, Mr Honer, it's easy," Jessie pressed.

Honer placed his mug behind the bale he was sitting on and rubbed his hands down his pants legs. They too were sweaty.

He stood and for the first time that night, looked at the folks who were dancing to the makeshift band who played makeshift music.

They started to play *Oh Danny Boy*, a new ballad that it seemed everyone knew. The square-dancing came to a halt and couples danced together, closer, touching.

Being short, Honer's face came just above Jessie's ample bosom, suitably covered, but he imagined those soft pillows nestling beneath the green dress she wore. The more he thought about them the more he sweated.

"You seem mighty hot, Mr Honer," Jessie said as a way of making conversation.

He raised his head and looked into her wide, innocent-looking eyes and he knew he had to have her. She would be the one. The first one.

★ ★ ★

Around midnight, the hoe-down began to break up as folks made their way back to their own farms and ranches. Tomorrow would be, like any other day, an early start: breakfast before sun up and out as the first rays of a new day began to lick across the land.

Honer was the last to leave. Being Saturday night, he had no work to attend to the following day. Half the hay bales were left for Hank and Jessie, as much as folks could spare, and there was some food and beer left, but the punch had long gone.

Watching Honer drive off in his fancy, red-leather seated buggy, Hank stood with his arm around his wife's waist and she his.

"This sure has got to be the best night ever," Hank said.

"The best," Jessie agreed. "It's like a new beginning."

"That's just what it is," Hank said. "Now, let's get to bed. We got an early start."

Jessie smiled up at her husband and they hugged. Hank turned out the oil-lamps bar one and together, they walked back towards the house happier than they'd been in a long, long time.

★ ★ ★

The drive back to Liberty was a long one that night for Bart Honer. His feelings were in turmoil — anger at the outcome of the barn-burning and a new sensation he hadn't felt since the death of his mother.

The night air felt cool on his still sweating face and the moon, full, lit up the prairie with an eery light-blue with shadows stark and black. A solitary elm stood by the side of the trail; its shadow duplicated it across the narrow track, and from beside it, Honer saw movement.

Reining in his horse, he tried to see into the blackness, but he couldn't discern anything. His spectacles began to steam up as a different sort of sweat now broke out: fear.

"Who, who's there?" he called out into the void.

There was no reply.

Honer sat, sweat pouring from his cold, fat body. Should he go on? Or, should he turn back?

He decided on the former.

The tree was set back off the track by some fifteen feet and, even with a full moon, it was impossible for him see anything with any clarity.

He set the horse to walking, all he could hear was the soft crunching as the wheels rolled across the hard-packed earth and the squeak of the leather seat as his weight shifted in rhythm with the motion of the buggy. Each sound seemed amplified out of all proportion. The sound of a coyote, baying at the moon, shot through the still night air like a shrieking cannon and Honer literally jumped out of his seat, heart beating like a drum.

Ten feet, eight feet, four feet, the tree loomed nearer. Pulling the side of his long jacket to one side, he gripped the butt of his Colt, owned for three years but never fired.

Was it loaded? Would it fire? These thoughts, too late to check up on, floated round his increasingly frenetic brain until he felt he had to scream.

From behind the tree trunk a figure appeared, standing half in and half out of shadow; a horse stood patiently behind him.

Honer swallowed hard, the dryness of his mouth now apparent. Pulling out his gun, he aimed it in a quivering hand towards the figure.

"I — I got you covered," he stammered.

The man neither moved nor spoke, he just stood where he was.

"What're you — after, mister?" Honer said again in a voice that quivered through the dark.

Again, the figure was silent and Honer could see a steely gaze from the man's eyes as the moon reflected in them.

Honer pulled at the trigger — hard. Nothing happened.

"You gotta release the safety," the voice said. The man, having spoken, turned and walked off behind the tree. As Honer watched, he mounted and, with a long stare back over his left shoulder, he raised his hand and rode off.

Fumbling frantically with the safety catch with fingers that didn't want to work, Honer did his best to loose off a shot — but to no avail. The man was too distant now anyway, and Honer was certain that, even if he had one of those fancy new repeating rifles, he couldn't hit him.

He followed the shape until the surrounding countryside swallowed him up, there was a faint shimmer, probably spurs as the moonlight struck them, and then he was gone.

With shaking hands, Honer replaced his useless sideiron, making a mental note to at least get some practice time in and grabbed a small, white handkerchief from his inside pocket to mop his brow.

Once his breathing had settled to somewhere approaching normal, he took his frustration out on the horse and, using the small whip, lashed onto the animal's back: "Giddup!" he yelled and continued his journey, not quite at a gallop, but not far off.

Hands still shaking, Honer inserted the large iron key into his front door and let himself in. First port of call was the whiskey bottle. He poured himself a large measure and knocked it back in one.

He wished he hadn't.

The sharp, acidic liquid burned through his throat before hitting his stomach like a lava flow and he coughed.

Taking a deep breath, he slowly calmed himself down. Living out in the Wild West, he thought, sure is gonna take some getting used to.

* * *

Dirk King rode on through the night. He'd camped out near a small creek in a hollow between some rocks. The night breezes missed his bed-roll and, when he'd lit the fire, he felt as snug as a bug in a rug.

He grinned to himself as he re-lived the scene at the elm tree: the scared look on Honer's face, the quivering voice, the shaking hands. Dang fool didn't even release the safety. He laughed out loud, the sound echoing through the rocky landscape.

The man, King thought, is a dang fool. Fifty bucks now maybe, but later, King knew he'd grow rich on the back of Honer. He may be a bank manager, but the man had no — what was the word that whore in Tucson had used? *Finesse*. Yeah, good word, French, she said. Finesse, the man lacked finesse.

Although Dirk King was a drifter, gunfighter whoremonger and killer, he was no fool. He'd seen right through Mr Honer and he knew he could beat him at his own game.

King leaned back against his saddle, cigarette perched between his lips and gazed up at the stars. He was going to be a rich man. A very, rich man.

3

THE late harvest was always a busy time of the year. Hands were in short supply — as was the money to pay them and the normal daily chores still had to be attended to.

Luke Garrett, Sheriff of Liberty, had his work cut out, too. He'd come up with no leads or clues in the past two weeks as to the reason for the Meadows' barn to suddenly burn down and Hank had been too busy to press him.

What Luke Garrett needed was a deputy, and what the town council had decided was that they couldn't afford one, so Luke was on his own.

Although not a large town as towns go, Liberty still had its fair share of crime; ranging from drunken brawls, for which Saturday was the favourite time, to robbery. Gunplay could and did happen at any time and for a variety of reasons.

As Luke left his small office opposite the bank, he set out on his normal night-time rounds. He checked the door to the bank first, locked as ever, then methodically checked both front and rear of the other buildings down that side of the main street before coming back up the other side.

The layout of Liberty was an L-shape, the saloon taking up the inside of the L, the livery stable taking up the outer corner, and where the street turned right, its name changed for some reason most folks had forgot. Main turned the corner and became Elm Street, and it was from Elm that Luke heard the shots.

Luke froze, not wanting to make any noise in case he missed something. The sound of hooves filled his ears but the horse was galloping away rather than towards him.

Pulling his gun from its holster, Luke

ran back onto Main and headed out towards Elm.

Peering round the corner of the now closed saloon, a first glance showed the street deserted, but as Luke scanned the area, he saw the dark lump lying to one side of Elm, near the water trough.

Keeping alert, his eyes now used to the dark, Luke crept forwards, edging closer to the body, but keeping his own body close to the building line, as he didn't want to get bushwhacked.

The town was as silent as the graveyard that Elm Street stopped at, at the eastern end of Liberty but Luke made no sudden moves, he listened and he waited.

As sure as he could be that the street was clear, Luke approached the fallen victim: it was Caleb Moss, owner of a two-bit homestead that backed on to the Meadows' place.

Caleb, fifty and a bachelor, seldom came into town, except to sell some of his produce and stock up on things he couldn't grow, tame or trap himself.

Luke checked him out: his wallet, never known to be ever full, was empty. He had two holes in his chest and still gripped tightly in his right hand was a pistol. Luke forced his fingers apart and released the weapon. He raised it to his nose and sniffed.

Cordite, and recent; the gun had been fired. Maybe, Luke thought, his killer might have taken a slug, too.

Turning Caleb onto his back, Luke went through his pockets: all empty.

"Shit!" Luke said out loud. "Killed fer a few dollars!"

Grabbing the body under each armpit, Luke dragged it back down Elm towards the livery stable; there'd be a buggy there he could use to get it up to Deke's place, Deke Wilmot being the doctor, vet and undertaker in Liberty.

Even in the cool, night air, Luke was sweating with the effort of towing the old man's heavy body. As he did so, he wondered why no one had so much as parted a curtain to see what all the shooting was about.

Sure, he reasoned, it was late, but some folks would still be up and about: then he remembered the hoe-down.

Reaching the livery stable, Luke pushed the door inwards with his back and towed Caleb behind him. Washington, the negro hostler, jumped out of his crib in the far corner of the stable as if it were full of scorpions.

"Who — who's that?" he stammered out.

In the gloom of the stable, Luke caught sight of the black man's eyes and teeth and smiled.

"It's me, Wash, Luke. Bin a killin'."

Washington Cartwright stepped forward and lit an oil-lamp and, raising it above his head, the yellow light filtered through the straw-dust filled air between the three men.

"Who dat bin a-killed?" Wash asked.

"Old Caleb, Caleb Moss," Luke replied, resting the body on the ground. "You got a buggy I kin use to get him over t'Deke's place?"

"Sure thing, Sheriff. Sure thing."

★ ★ ★

At the same time Dirk King leaned back on his saddle and settled down for the night out by the creek, so Bart Honer finished his whiskey.

He went back outside, unhitched and bedded his horse down for the night, placing a bag of barley over his nose, towed the buggy into the barn and locked his front door.

It felt good to be home. The air clammy and stuffy inside the small house soon disappeared when he opened up a window and Honer undressed and got into bed.

A thousand thoughts and ideas were swimming about his head, making sleep almost impossible.

Getting out of bed again, Honer went to his private desk and, unlocking the bottom drawer, took out copies of the accounts from the bank.

This would take his mind off Jessie Meadows, he thought, as he placed his spectacles on the end of his nose and pored over the papers.

Listed was everyone in the locale who had an account with the bank; their names, how much they owed, if anything, and whether the bank held a mortgage or not.

The only columns Honer was interested in were those who had started the steady, downwards spiral and had mortgaged, and in some cases, re-mortgaged their properties.

The name Meadows attracted his attention.

Property paid for outright but a mortgage for four thousand dollars taken out within six months.

A further loan of two thousand dollars a year later and now, Honer felt certain he would be getting a visit from Hank Meadows any day. The harvest wouldn't produce the amount of funds necessary to re-seed and see them through the winter months.

Honer ruled up a sheet of paper and listed three columns. The first column listed the names, the second the size of the property and its location and the third listed the amount of money they owed in relation to the bank's valuation of the property.

The name Meadows was the first on his list, followed by seven others: not in any particular order, but they all had a common boundary and when Honer checked the maps of the district, the Meadows' place was slap-bang in the centre.

Eyes sore, oil-lamp burning brightly, Honer sat at his desk for nearly three hours before he eventually climbed back into bed and slept the sleep of the innocent.

★ ★ ★

As did Dirk King. He'd decided to speed up the takeover plans of Honer, which Honer had thought to keep to himself, but Dirk had seen through the man. He knew what he was up to. If Honer reckoned on Dirk King being a fool, well, Dirk King would act the fool. He'd made up his mind on his own course of action, but *he* was keeping that to himself — two could play at that game.

Already, he'd sent a wire to get his old gang back together, the first time in three years since they split up after a bank heist had gone wrong. They'd escaped, but it was too close for comfort and they'd gone their separate ways.

The telegraph office had received a reply from Denver where both Kid Weaver and Brent Masters had headed. All he had to do was wait a while and, leaving the financing to Honer, Dirk figured him and his buddies would be rich men.

Dirk figured two days — tops, and they'd be here. In the meantime, he had a barn to burn, but this time, someone might just get themselves killed.

Stoking up the campfire, Dirk set the

coffee pot amidst the flames and lit a cigarette.

Fishing out some arrows, he began tying wadding near the barb. The wadding had been smeared with pitch, he found that pitch didn't burn itself out before the arrow hit its target.

By the time he'd fixed up three more arrows to add to the one he'd had left, the coffee was boiling. Pouring himself a cup, he sipped at the steaming black liquid and thought of the barn.

Brand spanking new, only finished the day before, he figured he might need all the arrows to get it afire, what with the wood being new.

Coffee and cigarette finished, Dirk kicked sand onto the fire and poured the coffee dregs atop that. He took his horse, tethered nearby, to the creek and let it drink while he saddled up.

Putting the bow and quiver over his shoulder, Dirk King mounted up and set off at a leisurely walking pace towards the Meadows' place. He was in no rush.

★ ★ ★

Hank and Jessie had been in the fields since first light. The corn, ripe and juicy was just begging to get picked and, with the help of some neighbours, they reckoned they'd get the corn in just before nightfall, if they were lucky.

Then, next day, they'd move on to whoever else needed a hand, which was practically most folks in these parts. By the end of the following week, everyone should have their last harvest of the year in, ready to ship out to the corn merchant who put in the highest bid.

Noon came, and with it, the heat of the day seemed to intensify and Jessie went down to the river to get the lemonade she'd made the day before. Work came to a halt for fifteen minutes while all and sundry slaked their thirst and ate bread and cheese to keep them going till they got home.

"'Bout twenty acres to go," Hank said. "May just get it in afore nightfall."

"I hope so," Jessie said, wiping the

sweat from her brow. "We got six more fields to do yet, and they're all bigger than ours."

"Don't remind me," Hank said. "My back's fit to bustin' right now. I'll concentrate on these last twenty afore I think about tomorrow."

With that, they all got back to work, hoping the price of corn would stay high enough to maybe have a little left when they'd settled their bills in town.

★ ★ ★

Bart Honer sat up in bed with a start. He'd been dreaming and it all seemed so real. There he was with that Meadows woman, laughing and joking and she was telling him how much she loved him and they were just about to have their first kiss when there was a knock on the door and . . .

Bart Honer woke up.

His initial disappointment was quickly dispelled as he wondered if the knocking was real or in the dream.

The hammer blows on his front door came again.

It was real.

Donning his fancy dressing-gown, Honer stumbled towards the front door.

"Who is it?" he called out, unwilling to just open the door.

"Weaver an' Masters," came the reply.

"Who are you?"

"Got a wire from Dirk King. You know where he is? He tole us to look you up."

Honer unlocked the front door and opened it wide. Outside stood two men. Both tall and dark with enough stubble on their faces to fill a bucket.

Their clothes were covered in trail dust and the smell that accompanied them almost made Honer gag.

Both men were armed to the teeth: their low-slung pistols, strapped to their thighs looked as if they'd had plenty of use. Behind them stood two raggedy horses that looked as if they'd been running all night.

The thing that sent a shiver down Honer's spine was the look in both men's eyes. Although they both wore smiles on their lips, their eyes were as dead as anything Honer could imagine. They stared at him with those dark, unblinking eyes and Honer knew instinctively that these two men were killers.

"I — I — don't know where Mr King is," he managed to get out, trying to keep his voice even — and failing. "Sometimes, he — he stays out by the creek. Sometimes, well, he don't."

"Place here we can eat?" Weaver asked.

"Sure. Yes. Yes, the saloon. Back down the street aways, on the far corner. Should be open now."

The two men turned as if to go but Masters turned back: "If'n you see Dirk, you be sure to tell him we're here."

"Yes. Sure thing. I'll tell him," Honer said and a cold sweat broke out all over his body.

He watched as the two men ambled back to their animals, mounted up and, without a glance back, walked their horses down Main Street.

Quickly closing the door, Honer mopped his brow. *What the hell is King playing at? Why has he got those two killers in town?*

Bart Honer had no idea. One thing he knew for sure: he didn't like it. Not one bit.

* * *

Lazily, Dirk King stepped out of his saddle.

He struck a match on his gunbelt and lit up a cigarette, inhaling deeply as he surveyed the surrounding countryside.

Lush fields of corn blazed off in all directions, the breeze swaying the heavy heads from side to side in never-ending motion. A beautiful sight — if you were

44

a farmer — to Dirk King, it was a funeral pyre.

Finishing his cigarette, he flicked it nonchalantly into the air, watching as the dull red end sent small sparks out that died as soon as they left it. The cigarette landed on the ground and a very faint white line of smoke rose into the air before being whisked off by the never-ending breeze.

King yawned lazily. Anyone seeing the man would assume he was about to lie down in the lush grass that surrounded the corn field and commune with Mother Nature.

Reaching for his bow, he carefully laid it on the ground before removing the quiver and its lethal contents. Selecting an arrow, he held it out in front of him — closing one eye and peering down the smooth, wooden shaft — assuring himself it was straight and true.

He checked the pitch-soaked wadding, making sure it was tight and, licking finger and thumb, he ran his hand over the flight feathers. He reached down and picked up the bow. The weight of it in his left hand felt good, it belonged there. Gripping the hand-hold on the bow, he placed the arrow between bow and thumb and with his right hand slotted the end of the arrow across the taut bow-string.

Adjusting his stance and shoulders, he pulled back the bow string, feeling the power of the bow as wood and string became rigid. Relaxing the bow, he held it in his left hand and with his right, he reached into his vest pocket and brought out a hand-made match.

Feeling the breeze on his face, King struck the match on his gunbelt and ignited the wadding. Taking careful, yet quick aim, allowing for the wind, he shot off the first arrow.

4

THE long, backbreaking day was drawing to a close. Already, the bright yellow glow of the sun was sinking and changing its colour as it sank lower and lower as it set in in the western sky. The orange-red glow that lit the prairie was brighter than usual and Hank was the first to notice.

Mopping his brow for the umpteenth time, he raised his eyes away from the rapidly diminishing corn and saw smoke.

"Fire!" he yelled. "Fire!"

Everyone froze gazing in the direction of Hank's pointing finger.

"Jesus, looks like your place, Hank!"

The voice carried with it Hank and Jessie's worst fears.

"Come on," Hank called out and immediately the seven people present downed tools and took to the buckboard.

They were thirty minutes from the Meadows' house and as they neared, Hank, standing in the rear of the buckboard, spoke quietly.

"It's the barn."

He hung his head, chin almost resting on his chest. Jessie held his hand, tightly.

But it wasn't just the barn. To the north of the Meadows' barn, a whole field of grass and corn was also ablaze. The air was thick with cloying white smoke and sparks were sent shooting up into the air.

There was nothing anyone could say or do, except to wait until the flames burned themselves out.

Then the wind changed.

"Goddamnit," Hank whispered, "the house!"

Arnie Dillon was the first to react positively.

"I got blasting powder," he shouted. "Use for tree stumps. If'n we can create a fire break, well, we just might save the house."

Arnie jumped atop his horse, tethered to the buckboard and set off at a gallop for his own barn. Within twenty minutes he was back.

"I reckon if we can set this off on the east side of the barn, we can create a fire break that should stop it," he said. "Anything that comes across, well, we can take care of that."

Without further ado, the men set about their task. As they neared the rear of the barn, the heat and smoke was intense and with the freshening wind, it was all they could do to breathe.

"I got five barrels," Arnie yelled. "Space 'em out, 'bout fifteen feet apart, that should do it."

Bandannas wrapped tightly round their faces kept some, but not all, of the smoke from clogging their lungs, but the heat was the worst. Nothing they had could shield them from that.

Hank's biggest worry was the blasting powder blowing up in his hands. "Keep your backs to the flames," he yelled above the roar of the flames. "Try an' protect the powder."

The smoke billowed all around them, making visibility practically nil. Working blindly, the men set the barrels of blasting powder in place without mishap. All Arnie had to do now was set the fuses and then run like hell.

* * *

Dirk King entered the saloon and ordered a bottle of whiskey and a glass. He grabbed them off the counter and walked to the far corner of the small room. Selecting a table that gave him an unrestricted view of the entrance, he sat, pulled the cork out of the whiskey bottle with his teeth and spat it on the sawdust-covered floor. Filling the small glass, he downed the fiery liquid in one go and re-filled the glass, sinking half this time.

The warm, burning glow that emanated from his stomach filled his entire body. The rough whiskey did its job, relaxing and warming and making him feel slightly light-headed.

Pleased with his day's work, King intended to get drunk and maybe have a bowl of chili and bread to mop it up with. The whiskey was going down well — too well — and King thought about ordering some food before he got too drunk.

Ambling across the room to the long bar set on one side of the saloon, he ordered his favoured bowl of chili and was about to return to his table when a voice cut through the room.

"Hold it right there, mister."

King stood where he was, his back to the direction from which the voice had come.

"Nice an' easy, now. Turn round."

King, his right arm hanging loosely at his side, fingers twitching to get a hold of his Colt, turned as he was ordered. By the time he'd completed the turn, his gun was drawn and cocked, aimed at whoever was seeking to take him out.

In front of him stood a grinning Kid Weaver and an openly laughing Brent Masters.

"Sure put the shit up you," Weaver said, slapping his thigh in amusement.

"Sure took your time gettin' here," King said. "Another second an' I'd blown that stupid grin right off'n your face." King released the hammer and reholstered his weapon.

"Hell, boy, you's a-slippin'. Time was when you'd never get caught cold turkey'd like that," Masters chipped in.

"Two-bit shit hole like this? There ain't no one in town who's got the balls," King said and sat down at his table, waiting for Weaver and Masters to join him.

"'Tender, two more glasses an' two more chilis," King yelled across the saloon.

"You got it," the barkeep snapped back.

"So, what's the deal?" Weaver asked, not being a man who wasted much time on pleasantries.

"We got ourselves some easy pickin's here, boys," King began. "Seems we got a greedy bank manager who's gonna drive off the homesteaders and dirt farmers and ranchers who's in to owin' the bank money. I already burned down a barn or two and set some fields o' ripe corn alight."

"So, what's in it fer us?" Masters put in.

"No more bummin' round fer sure," King said. "This manager, Bart Honer, he don't figure I knows what he's up to. Paid me fifty dollars jus' to burn a barn down. I reckon we could end up ownin' some prime land hereabouts an' live out the rest of our lives in a mite o' comfort."

Their conversation was disrupted as the barkeep brought their food over. "Eat an' enjoy, gents," he said amiably and waddled back to the barcounter to resume the never-ending job of polishing up the glasses.

"Shit'll hit the fan soon," King continued. "What Honer don't know is I already set the ball rollin'. There's more goin' on than he realizes."

The three men set about their food with gusto.

* * *

The explosion that resulted from the blasting powder sent a rain of hot ash, dirt, rocks, and eventually dead corn heads landing everywhere. Luckily, no one was seriously injured, although one or two people would have bruises from the rocks for a few days.

The blast did the trick. There was no way of saving the barn; new wood or not, it had caught fire good and proper, but the blazing corn field was blown out making it easier for the group to douse the remaining flames with sacking and the odd bucket of water.

An hour later, smoke still billowing into the near dark sky, the men were able to relax.

★ ★ ★

The explosion was heard in town but only a muffled roar, loud enough for Luke Garrett to take notice. He'd reached Deke's place, a smallholding on the edge of town, but the old man wasn't there.

Luke had no choice. He left the body and the buggy tethered to the rail outside Deke's house and unhitched his horse. In the distance, the ominous black pall of smoke was visible in the night sky.

"Jesus H.," he muttered under his breath. "What now?"

Using his reins he lashed at the neck of his mount and set off at a gallop. From the direction of the smoke, Luke knew exactly where to head for: the Meadows' place again.

Thirty minutes later, Luke reined in

his animal and stared in disbelief at the rubble that was the new barn. Worse, this time, about forty acres of ripe corn had been set ablaze in the adjoining fields belonging to another farmer, the now dead Caleb Moss.

"Hank. What the hell's goin' on out here?" Luke asked as he dismounted near the group of exhausted men.

"Beats me, Luke. Someone's sure got it in for me," Hank replied and took a swig from his canteen.

"Everythin' gone?" Luke asked.

"Yup. Every damn thing. I don't know if'n I wanna start over agen," Hank said.

"I'll have a look-see," Luke said trying to sound encouraging.

"There ain't nothing *to* see." Hank responded. "A pile o' ashes is all there is. There ain't no way I can carry on now."

"You done it before, Hank," Luke said.

"Yeah. I done it before, but I can't expect folks to rally round for the second time in as many weeks. An' I sure can't do it by maself."

"Well, hang fire, Hank, if'n you'll pardon the expression. You'll be surprised what folks'll do in times of a crisis. Anyhows, I'll have a check round, see if I can come up with something." Luke mounted up and suddenly remembered Caleb.

"You seen Caleb recently?"

"Not that I can think of," Hank said. "Mind you, old Caleb keeps to himself."

"Caleb's dead, Hank. I found him earlier in town, gunned down. He loosed off a shot, but there's no sign of his attacker."

"Oh, no! Not Caleb!" Jessie had come to her husband's side and caught the bad news.

Hank held his wife tightly. "There's somethin' goin' on round here," he said between clenched teeth. "an' it's high time I did somethin' about it."

"Now don't you go going off half-cocked," Luke said. "I'm the law round here an' it's my job to take care o' things."

"Well, if'n you don't mind me sayin', Sheriff, you ain't done too good a job so far."

"Be warned, Hank. An' the rest o' you. There ain't gonna be no vigilantes in these parts, not while I'm Sheriff!"

"Well, Sheriff, *you* be warned. I ain't standin' by an' lettin' some no-goods burn me out! If'n you don't come up with the culprits, I sure will."

"I ain't gonna argue wuth you, Hank. Leave this to the law." Luke dug his heels in and rode off towards the smouldering barn. He couldn't blame Hank for feeling the way he did, but his conscience wouldn't allow no lynch mob.

The barn was smouldering and although Luke could feel the heat rising in the cooler night air, it wasn't that hot that he couldn't approach and stare into the ashes. Not that there was much to see, but a shiny object caught his eye.

Hunting round for a stick, Luke

knocked the object clear of the ashes and, wrapping a neckerchief round his hand, he picked it up.

"Well, I'll be," he said out loud. "Now where d'you 'spose this thing came from?"

Luke stared at the pointed object, blowing on it to cool it down before he slipped it into his vest pocket.

★ ★ ★

Monday morning was pretty much like any other in Liberty. The store opened up, along with the bank, and that was about it. Livery stable never closed, and the saloon only shut up shop when the last customer fell out.

Bart Honer sat at his desk, going through his private list. He licked his lips at the prospect of being his own boss. No more taking orders from central office. No siree. Pretty soon, he'd own all the land for as far as the eye could see. Fair an' square; well, almost, anyway, he reasoned.

After all, he thought, setting fire to one little barn wasn't such a bad thing. No one was injured or anything. It was just a barn.

Bart Honer could live with that.

Carefully putting his list in his inside pocket, he set about the day's business. Two minutes later, Dirk King entered the bank, along with the two men he'd met the day before.

Honer broke out in a sweat. The three men just stood staring at him. He motioned them through and they followed him into his tiny office.

"What do you want?" Honer asked.

"Jus' thought I'd keep you up to date," King began. "Seems like one o' your farmers met with an accident, last night."

"An accident? What sort of accident?" Honer asked, dreading the reply.

"Seems like my gun went off an' he was standin' in the way," Dirk replied, keeping his face straight, which was more than Weaver and Masters could do.

"You — you killed him?" Honer said.

"Hell, no. He just died with two o' my bullets in his chest." He paused before adding in a matter-of-fact tone, "Oh, an' you know that new barn out to the Meadows' place?"

"What about it?"

"Well, it ain't there no more."

This time King grinned, showing even white teeth.

Honer stared at King for a second or two. All his plans, his dreams of acquiring property without a soul being injured, went out the window.

"Oh my God!"

"Well he sure ain't ours," King said and the three men giggled like schoolboys.

"What have you done?" Honer said uselessly.

"Hell, I was only followin' your orders, *Mr* Honer. Seems like you owe me."

"I didn't ask you to burn the barn down again."

"Makes no dif'rence to me," King said. "I figure you want that place. Ain't that right *Mr* Honer? Ain't that the reason you wanted the first barn burned out?"

Honer stared at the man he'd badly misjudged. Seems he wasn't a no-good, brainless cow-poke after all.

He had to think. It wasn't his idea to kill anyone, so how could anyone blame him? They couldn't. It wasn't his fault if this thug decided to take matters into his own hands, was it? No, of course it wasn't.

Besides, it might speed things up a tad.

"Who 'accidentally' died?" Honer eventually asked.

"Kinda wondered when you'd get around to askin' that," King said with a leer on his face. "Man named Moss, Caleb Moss. He got — he had — the land that sides onto the Meadows' place."

Honer's brain raced. Did this man know more than he was letting on?

Honer doubted it, but he sure knew more than Honer had figured he would.

"All right, Mr King. How much do I owe you?"

"Well, that kinda depends," King said.

"Depends? Depends on what?" Honer said, getting nervous.

"How far you's plannin' to go. Ain't that right, boys?"

Weaver and Masters nodded, although they weren't clear, exactly, what King was going on about.

"I don't know what you mean," Honer said.

"What I mean, Mr Honer, is that I figure on takin' a parcel o' that land myself. Me an' my boys here, I figure you an' me ought to be partners."

"Partners!" Honer wiped sweat from his face.

"You heard. Brain an' brawn, Mr Honer. Brain an' brawn." King laughed and turned on his heel.

"We'll be in touch, Mr Honer. An'

just in case you feel like pullin' out now, remember, I got a tale I can tell the Sheriff, an' I can be long gone."

Honer went as white as a sheet as the three men left his office. This would take some serious thinking, he thought. Very serious thinking.

5

"**I** AIN'T got no choice," Hank said as he strapped on his gunbelt. He opened the foot locker by the side of their bed and removed a sack-covered object. Carefully untying the string, he revealed a Winchester repeater.

Hank sat at the table and began wiping off the excess oil round the barrel and stock. Satisfied, he cocked the rifle and checked that it was empty, before raising it to his shoulder and gently squeezing the trigger.

The action was smooth. The hammer hit home with precision, the sound it made was in a strange way comforting.

"Please, Hank," Jessie went on. "You heard what Luke said. Leave it up to the law."

"I cain't do that, Jessie," Hank said gruffly. "The law ain't doin' enough.

We already had two barns burned down, now old Caleb's been shot dead. Someone is out to ruin, not only us, but our friends and neighbours, too. I cain't allow that to happen."

Hank loaded up the shells into the breech of the Winchester until he could get no more in. Leaning it against the table, he took his Colt Peacemaker out of its holster and checked the barrel: six slugs loaded, safety on. He reholstered the weapon and grabbed his hat.

"What about me?" Jessie pleaded. "What do I do if you get yourself killed?"

"I don't aim to do that," Hank said. "What I aim to do is find out who's behind this. I want you to head into town and stay put 'til I come for you."

Without saying another word, Hank looked at his wife square in the eyes, then he lowered them, and left their home.

Jessie watched as he mounted up, placing the rifle in its scabbard behind the saddle. She stood on the small verandah, arms folded — not in anger, but apprehension. She stood and wondered if this was the last she would see of her man.

* * *

Apart from eating and drinking, there wasn't much a band of gunslinging drifters could do in Liberty. There was no whorehouse, and they certainly didn't want a job.

King, Weaver and Masters left the bank and headed straight back to the saloon.

"You figure he'll buy it?" Master asked.

"He ain't got no choice. Either he does, or he's dead. Either way, we ain't gonna lose out. Let's eat."

They sat at a table at the back of the saloon, making sure they were out of earshot.

"Now," King began, "I don't reckon the sheriff's up to much use in these parts. He ain't come up with nothin' so far," King grinned. "Mind you, I ain't left him nothin' to come up with."

"What you plannin' on next, Dirk?" Weaver asked.

"Torchin' a few more fields," he answered straight away. "Reckon them dirt farmers ain't got the wherewithal to carry on once their harvest has bin destroyed. Once they's flat busted, it'll be easy to buy 'em out fair an' square."

"When we goin'?" Master asked.

"Soon's we've had some chow. We got plenty o' time." King banged on the table attracting the attention of the barkeep who'd been out back as they'd entered.

"What'll it be, gents?" he called.

"We'll have some, eggs, easy over, ham and coffee," King said without bothering to ask the other two men what they wanted.

"Comin' right up." The barkeep went back into the small storeroom that doubled as a kitchen and the three men could hear the clanking around as the frypan was placed on the stove.

"Kid, as soon as we've done here, I want you to high-tail over to the store and get some lamp oil, much as you can carry. I figure we'll hit a couple o' fields afore nightfall. The Meadows' place is fairly central, old Honer sure wants that piece o' land badly, so we'll fire some o' the surrounding. Make it a mite easier."

King leant back in his chair and lit up a cigarette. "Hell, you better git some matches, too," he added and laughed. "Wouldn't do to have no light now would it?"

Their conversation was brought to a halt as the barkeep brought out their food and coffee.

"Hey, you got any biscuits?" Weaver asked.

"Hell, yes. Finest in town," came the reply.

"Then bring us a bunch," Weaver said, his mouth already full of eggs and ham.

Breakfast over, the three left separately: King to ride back to the creek, Weaver to the general store, and Masters to the horses.

Dan Grover didn't bat an eyelid as Kid Weaver bought two barrels of oil and a dozen boxes of matches, he didn't bat an eyelid when he bought ten cartons of .45 slugs, either. Weaver paid for his purchases and left the store to join Masters outside and, together, they rode out of Liberty to meet up with Dirk King.

* * *

Luke Garrett rode into town as the three gunslingers rode out. He rode on up to the livery stable and checked his horse in, then walked across to the jailhouse.

The coffee tasted like mud, but it was hot and wet and he was grateful.

Luke went through the file of Wanted posters, but nothing grabbed him. There weren't many strangers around town but those that were there didn't match up to any of the artist's impressions he scanned. The more Luke looked at the posters the more he doubted *anyone* could look like the drawings.

He fished in his vest pocket and brought out the shiny metal object he'd found out at Hank Meadows' barn. Still with a small fragment of wood attached, it had been a long time since Luke had seen an arrow head. But he sure was looking at one now.

He'd spent time out at both barn fires looking in the vicinity for any tracks that shouldn't have been there, but, in the general confusion, the ground had been well churned up. He moved out further, looking for tracks that maybe stopped short of the compound and then turned away again, but he'd found nothing.

The arrow head could be a reason for that, he figured. A man could stay well away from both barn and compound with a flaming arrow, providing he knew how to use the bow, of course.

What the hell was goin on? he thought to himself. Two fires — three if you counted the corn field, and the killing of Caleb Moss. What could anyone stand to gain by burning down a barn? It sure beat the hell out of Luke Garrett.

He walked across the small room to the wood stove and poured himself the last dregs of the coffee. It was bitter, thick and black, he almost had to chew it to swallow it. Hell, he thought, I gotta make some fresh.

The water pitcher was empty and, as there was no pump nearby, he wandered over to the saloon to get some. At least it would be fresh from their pump.

"Howdy, Sheriff."

Samuel K. Vermont, barkeeper, cook, chief bottle-washer and owner of the No-Name saloon, greeted Luke as he entered.

"Sam. Fill up the pitcher for me?" Luke asked.

"Sure thing. Anything else?"

"Yeah. I know it's early, but if your beer's cold I need to wash out the trail dust and the coffee I've had brewing all night."

"Know what you mean. Mite dry myself, I think I'll join you."

Sam filled the pitcher, then brought two mugs of beer round the front and sat at one of the tables. The saloon was deserted. No one even eating breakfast and, as this was the only place to eat, Luke figured old Sam was having a hard time making a living these days.

"So, what's new?" Sam asked.

"Nothing that you don't already know," Luke said.

Samuel K. Vermont knew *everything* that went on in and around Liberty, sometimes he knew things *before* they even happened.

"No nearer discoverin' who fired the barns, then?"

"Who said they had bin?" Luke asked, suddenly interested.

"I do. Stands to reason. Barn *can*

catch fire o' course, bin known t' happen. But *twice*? No siree. You ask my opinion, they was burned down on purpose." Sam took a mighty swig of his beer, draining half the glass in one go.

"You reckon, huh?" Luke said.

"Sure do. No other reason fits."

"An' who'd you reckon did it then?" Luke asked.

"Well, that's a tough one. Could be anyone," Sam said.

"Don't reckon so myself," Luke countered. "Man burns down a barn an' sets fire to a field o' ripe corn, what's in it fer him?"

Sam rubbed his chin, scratched his balls and thought for a while.

"Danged if I know," he said finally and finished off his beer.

"Seen any strangers round town?"

"Yup. Had three in earlier. Had themselves a breakfast an' then left. Why?"

"Sam, for a smart man you sure ask some dumb questions."

"Oh, right. You figure it's strangers, huh?"

"Well, I don't reckon Hank burned his own barn down, an' old Caleb sure as hell didn't shoot hisself, an' unless there's someone in town bearin' a grudge that no one else knows about, yeah, I figure it's strangers."

"Hell, Luke, there's always plenty o' folks passin' through Liberty. Specially at this time o' the year. Looking for casual work out in the fields, most of 'em. Earn enough money to buy a few drinks an' then move on."

"Well you sure as hell should know. There ain't nowhere else to get a drink in this town," Luke replied, finishing his beer.

"Let me get you another, on the house."

"Thanks, Sam. Then I gotta go."

Sam pulled two more glasses of beer and the old friends sat in silence while they drank them.

"Thanks, Sam. I'll catch you later."

"Good luck, Luke. If'n I hear

anything, you'll be the first to know."

"'Preciate it, Sam."

Luke left the saloon, but he had no idea where to go or what to do, and he didn't like that feeling.

* * *

Jessie Meadows stood on the verandah and fixed her eyes on her husband's back until she could no longer see him. Part of her sympathized and understood his reaction. But most of her didn't want him taking the law into his own hands.

There must be something I can do to stop him, she thought. But what?

She had to tell Luke. Having made up her mind on a course of action, she felt better. Readying herself, she donned her best bonnet, rigged up the team, and set off for town. Maybe Luke could talk some sense into him, she thought.

The morning air was still fresh but already Jessie could feel the warmth of the sun on her back and she knew that within an hour or two the freshness would be burned away and the air would become hot and burn the back of your throat every time you breathed in.

The ride to town, she knew, would take her half an hour. No sense in tiring out the animals by galloping. She decided that as soon as the trail in passed near the creek, she'd water the animals and give them a short rest before heading into town.

She gazed around the valley; to the north the mountains, soon to be snow capped stood out like huge purple boulders on the horizon. In front of them, prairie lands, rich enough in grass to feed a couple of thousand steers for a hundred years or more. To the south, the farmland. Rich, fertile and well watered, despite being on the edge of a desert that filled her eyesight to the horizon in the east. She never ceased to be amazed how beautiful the land was. Hard, but giving.

Liberty lay north-east and pretty soon she'd pass across the creek at the Old Ford. A rock bed cut a swathe through the grasslands and the water spread as it passed across it, making crossing easy. A small outcrop to her left told her she was getting near and the animals pricked up their ears and noses as the smell of the sweet, cold water filled the air.

Atop the outcrop, stood a lone tree and at the very top of that tree stood a nest, resting precariously how, she knew not. A giant tangle of twigs and branches carefully and expertly interlaced forming a home every bit as stable as her own.

She could see the pair of golden eagles even from this distance, the sunlight catching their heads and reflecting now and then off their beaks and twinkling, black-brown eyes.

Of all God's creatures, thought Jessie, the eagle was her favourite. Proud, independent, brave and just plain beautiful.

As she neared the Ford, the pair took to the air. Not, she knew, because she was approaching, they weren't scared of her. No, they'd seen something to eat and they were off hunting. She watched as, with seemingly little effort, they gained height and then lazily glided through the air, the small flight feathers at the very tip of their wings making minor adjustments as they wheeled lower and lower until one of the birds dived head-first at the ground.

Jessie smiled to herself. Whatever they were after, they sure have caught.

She reached the ford and reined in the team, and straight away both animals began lapping at the clear, cool water.

Jessie never heard a thing. One minute she was standing by the team, gazing up high at the lone bird, the next, she felt a sharp pain to the back of her neck and she fell like a stone in the water.

★ ★ ★

Hank Meadows had no idea where he was headed or what he was going to do. He'd visited three neighbours, telling them of his intention to capture whoever it was that had targetted his ranch and probably killed Caleb Moss.

Sympathetic though the neighbours were, they were in no position to ride with him. They had their corn to harvest and, more importantly, they weren't shootists.

Hank decided to find high ground and wait. He'd already figured that, since his own place had been torched and Caleb was dead anyway, at least those two homesteads were safe, or at least he could see no reason why they should be attacked again.

The first attack had been in the dead of night, but the second had been in daylight, making it a hard job to stand guard twenty-four hours a day without any help.

It seemed pointless riding around the

prairie aimlessly, in the hope of maybe riding across the culprits, so Hank decided to keep watch over the valley from the rocks to the north of his own place. At least that way, he reasoned, if he saw smoke, he could be on the scene pretty quick — he hoped.

Heading off now with some purpose and a definite plan in mind made Hank feel more useful.

Reaching the higher ground, he scouted round for a good vantage point that would also give him cover. Satisfied with his choice, he dismounted, watered his animal, and took out his bedroll. He thought about lighting a fire to boil up some coffee, but decided against it. There was no way he wanted *anyone* to know he was up there.

Settling himself as comfortably as he could, he sat and waited.

6

JESSIE MEADOWS opened her eyes
to blackness. She'd been blindfolded
and it took her a few seconds
to realize. The back of her head
throbbed as if she'd been . . . Then
she remembered. She'd felt a bang
on the back of her head and that
was the last thing she remembered
— until now.

She could hear no voices, all she
could hear was the gentle trickle of
water. She must still be near the creek,
she thought.

She kept perfectly still, flexing her
wrists to see how tight the ropes that
bound her were. She had movement.
Carefully, and much calmer than she
would have thought, she twisted her
wrists until she worked one of the
ropes over her left hand. Now, with
one hand free, it was a simple matter

to slip her right hand out.

She still didn't move a muscle. She had no way of knowing if she were being guarded or not. Imperceptibly, she moved her legs, they were free. Now, she thought, what do I do?

Straining her ears until she thought they'd burst, she listened.

Still nothing.

She began to breathe deeply, calming herself down, readying herself.

Slowly, she brought her left hand from behind her and moved up to the blindfold.

Still silence.

Hooking her thumb under the rough cloth, she pulled it down.

The pain as the sunlight hit her left eye was excruciating. She could see nothing except a bright white light. Gradually, her eye got used to the brightness and began to focus in on the surrounding countryside.

She pulled the blindfold off and waited a while with closed eyes until the bright red light behind her eyelids settled and her head stopped throbbing a little.

She was lying by the creek in a secluded hollow surrounded by rocks. At her feet was the remains of a campfire, the soot-blackened coffee pot still in the ashes.

Looking left and right, she found she was alone. Whoever had bushwhacked her didn't figure on her coming round so quickly, otherwise, she thought, she'd be guarded.

Who in tarnation had slugged her?

She didn't dwell on that thought. Whoever it was might return soon so the quicker she got herself out of there, the better.

Leaning on one elbow, she slowly regained her feet. Swaying slightly as her head swam, she steadied herself and began to walk towards the ford hoping against hope that the buckboard and team was still there.

They were, and she breathed a sigh of relief. She didn't think she had the strength to walk to town or return home. The two animals still had their noses in the water and without a timepiece, Jessie had no idea how long she'd been unconscious but, from the position of the sun, she figured no more than an hour, if that.

Climbing atop the buckboard, she grabbed the reins and set off once more towards Liberty, wishing now that she had a weapon of some sort — just in case.

* * *

The town was quiet, folks going about their normal midday chores. Most people stayed inside at what was the hottest part of the day, but there were those that couldn't. Sam Vermont swept the boardwalk outside of the saloon, not that it needed it, but if someone happened to ride through or walk past, he'd be able to have a conversation which might pass a couple of minutes.

No one did though, so as soon as

he'd finished, he went back inside the empty saloon.

Luke gazed out of the jailhouse window at the deserted street. Tumbleweed ran down Main and got stuck outside the livery stable and, as Luke looked on, Washington came out and kicked it free, sending it down Elm Street to come to a rest at the cemetery.

Dan Grover sat outside his store smoking a pipe and reading a month-old newspaper or magazine that he'd probably already read cover to cover, but the next stage wasn't due through for another week or so, so he'd read it over and over until the stage brought more news from the outside world.

Dan liked nothing more than telling the rest of the community, especially those who couldn't read or write, what was happening out there. And he did that at every opportunity.

Luke gazed at the sky: clear blue, not a cloud in sight. A breeze, hot and dry, ran through Liberty at a constant speed. He knew that, within a month, the breeze would turn to a wind, the heat would dry up and the first stages of a quick fall that would run on into winter would transform the landscape.

With luck, rain would fall, filling the already deep-dug wells and swelling the river. The mountains clearly visible would be snow-capped and come spring, the old creek would flood again, filling the prairie with cold snow-melted water and when that had been soaked up by the ever-thirsty land, the farmers would start the annual cycle all over again.

But that was a long way off and Luke's mind quickly returned to the job in hand. The peace and serenity of Liberty and the surrounding countryside was at odds with the killing and burnings and Luke just didn't know where to start.

The door opened and Deke Wilmot walked in, bright and breezy as ever. "Luke," he said and, without waiting for an invitation, poured himself a coffee and sat on the chair facing Luke's desk.

"Howdy, Deke," Luke said and poured himself a coffee too.

"That body outside my house your doin'?" Deke asked.

"Caleb Moss, yeah, I left him there, couldn't find you."

"Been out aways overnight. Damn baby took forever to deliver an' I had to grab me some shuteye. Then one o' the cows decided to drop one, too. I tell you, Luke, there ain't no peace for the wicked." Deke laughed and sipped at his coffee.

"You had a look at Caleb?" Luke asked.

"What's to look at? Two slugs, .45s, smack bang in the chest. Man died instantly," Deke said in a matter-of-fact tone.

"Guess the town council'll pay for the funeral," Luke said. "Recoup the money when the farm's sold off."

"No problem. I got a box ready. He ain't got no kin so I'll bury him later today when the heat of the sun's died down a tad."

"Okay. You want a hand?" Luke asked.

"Hell, no. Hole's dug already. You know who killed him?"

"Nope. Not a clue. Heard the shots and found the body."

"Heard the Meadows' place got hit," Deke said.

"Bad news sure travels fast round here."

"Quicker'n a tornado in the fall," Deke said and laughed.

The two men chatted amiably for a few more minutes before Deke made a move.

"I'll catch you later, Luke," he said.

"Sure, Deke. I'm trying to figure out what's goin' on, an' gettin' nowhere fast."

★ ★ ★

Bart Honer was poring over the deeds to Caleb Moss's homestead. The bank owned it lock, stock and barrel. Caleb had been in a bad way. The drought of last year had affected him more than the rest of the farmers even though they'd all rallied round trying to help him out, he'd lost two crops and was on the edge. Now he was over the edge and Honer licked his lips in anticipation.

No need to use a phoney name, he thought to himself, place was only worth a few thousand dollars and Honer had more than enough money stashed to cover that.

As the manager, it was up to him to get the best price possible to offset the bank's losses; as the purchaser, he'd pay rock-bottom.

The mortgage was to the tune of three-thousand dollars, much too high a price. If Honer had been manager when the mortgage was taken out he would have foreclosed there and then. But he wasn't in Liberty then. He sure was now.

He drafted up two phoney bids, each

ridiculously low, and then his own bid. He topped the price by three hundred dollars, no need to be extravagant, and lodged the papers.

Signing on the dotted line, he transferred one thousand seven hundred dollars into the bank's account and he was a landowner.

Placing all the documents into the safe, he kept the deeds out, these he'd keep at home in his locked drawer.

Caleb Moss had no relatives, and he'd died owing the bank. He came into this world with nothing and he left with even less.

Business had been slow in the bank and Honer took out his pocketwatch: a quarter after three. Time to shut up shop, he thought.

The door was slammed open and in strode Dirk King and two partners.

"What now, Mr King? What now?"

King smiled at Honer and slowly struck a match and lit a long cheroot that was dangling from his lips. Puffing out a cloud of smoke, he kept the match burning, never taking his eyes off Honer.

He dropped the match into a waste basket and the crumpled paper that filled it burst into flame.

"What do you think you're doing?" Honer cried out. "Are you mad?" He jumped up and poured the dregs of his coffee in the burning basket and then grabbed the pot to extinguish it completely. The smell of burning paper filled the bank and Honer coughed.

"Jes to let you see how accidents happen, Mr Honer," King said and his two buddies laughed.

"What do you want?" Honer asked again.

"Me an' the boys are a bit short o' foldin' money. That old man didn't carry much an' we gotta live, *Mr Honer.*"

King sat opposite Honer's desk, leaned back and put his booted feet atop the highly polished surface.

"'Sides, we got expenses," King continued. "We've already laid out for oil an' stuff. It don't come cheap, Honer."

"How, how much do you need?" Honer asked.

"Need? Now that's a different story to how much we want, Honer," King drawled. "I reckon five hundred'll see us clear for awhiles."

"Five hundred! Are you crazy?"

King jumped up and grabbed Honer by the lapels of his jacket, the burning end of his cheroot inches from Honer's face.

"Now the first time you said that, I was willin' to ignore it. Now you said it agen, an' that makes me real mad, Honer. You go to your safe an' git the money an' if I figure I need more, you'll git that too, got it?"

Honer nodded. His face had reddened as King's grip tightened, almost choking him.

"Yes, I'll — I'll get it now," he managed to answer.

"Now that's more like it *Mr* Honer. See, I tole you boys he was an all right kinda guy," King laughed and released Honer's coat.

Honer almost fell to the ground, his legs were shaking like a leaf in a high wind. Taking out a 'kerchief he mopped his always sweating brow and crossed the room to the safe.

A wet patch appeared at his crotch as fear released a stream of hot liquid and Honer felt it run down his legs and into his shoes.

"Well I'll be," King laughed, "you dang pissed yourself, Mr Honer!"

Honer couldn't get any redder than he already was and he grinned selfconsciously without raising his eyes to King's.

"You better get on home an' change your pants, Honer, afore somebody sees what you's done."

Honer handed the wad of dollar bills over to King without saying a word.

"Good man," King said. "I'll be in touch, Mr Honer, real soon."

The three men left the bank laughing and Honer swore he'd get his revenge.

He didn't know how — yet — but he was determined.

King and his gang rode out of Liberty, after stocking up on whiskey, and headed back to the creek. Now they had some money, they all wanted a piece of the woman they'd left there.

"Whiskey and a woman, boys," King said, "best combination a man can have, less'n it's two women."

All three laughed loudly as they left town.

★ ★ ★

Jessie Meadows was regaining her strength — and her senses. She pulled off the trail and unhitched one of the horses. She told herself off for being so stupid as to stick to a trail when whoever had slugged her could be riding on towards her.

Making sure the buckboard was safely hidden, she left a bag of feed for the remaining horse and set off for Liberty cutting a wide arc round the main trail. It might take an extra hour to get to town, but, she thought, at least I'll get there.

Riding bareback wasn't the most comfortable of positions to find herself in. Each time the horse put hoof to ground, a fresh wave of throbbing erupted in her head, making her feel nauseous and giddy at the same time. She tried to think of other things, but the uncomfortable ride and the heat soon began to have an effect.

Jessie was not a weak woman. Slight as she was, she was a hard and capable worker and had never fainted in her life. But as she rode on, the giddiness began to get worse and, to add insult to injury, she began to get double vision.

Holding on tightly to the horse's mane, she fought the nausea, trying to concentrate on getting to town. She thought she'd succeeded, but as she looked ahead, the horse appeared to have two heads. A wave of sickness swept over her, her breath came in short pants and sweat ran down her face until she could taste it.

Her strength seemed to fade away and her brain was telling her to let go and rest but she fought hard against it, trying to breathe deeply and repeating out loud: "Ride on, ride on, ride on!"

Just as it seemed that she had won, a wave of blackness swept over her and she saw her hands release the mane and watched as the ground came up to meet her.

She landed heavily, rolled over once and was still.

The horse galloped on for a few yards before realizing that no one was making him run, so he stopped and began to graze idly on the sweet grass without a care in the world.

7

THE funeral was a simple affair. Deke Wilmot issued the death certificate, cleaned up the corpse, supplied the coffin and presided at the service.

A small knot of ten people attended and, as soon as the coffin hit the ground, they quickly disappeared anxious to get on with their work.

"I'll give you a hand to fill it in, Deke," Luke said.

"Hell, no. Wash'll take care o' that later. Thirsty work though," Deke added. "Reckon I'll go chew the fat with Sam over to the saloon, he'll be about ready to open now."

"Okay, but I think I'll give that one a miss. Thinkin' o' takin' a ride out round the valley. Keep my eyes skinned."

"You take care, Luke," Deke said

as he walked back down Elm to the saloon.

Luke watched him go and then mounted his horse. The sun was beginning to set once more on Liberty and Luke figured there was an hour, maybe an hour-and-a-half of daylight left.

At least there's been no killings or burnings this Monday, and with a bit of luck, Luke thought, it might be the end of it.

He wheeled his animal around and set off at a steady canter, scanning the prairie for signs of smoke and relieved when he saw none.

He decided to call out at Hank and Jessie's first. The arrowhead was in his vest pocket and he wanted to see if Hank ever used a bow and arrow, though for what Luke had no idea. If Hank didn't own one, then whoever burned the barns down sure did.

He followed the southern trail out to Hank's place; that trail weaved its way through the corn fields before coming out on the prairie to the north. The creek was low so there'd be no difficulty crossing higher up and taking a short-cut across Caleb's place.

The ride out to the Meadows' place was usually a pleasure for Luke. A nice couple, he thought, and they always made him welcome. But when he'd last seen Hank, the man seemed at the end of his tether. Luke just hoped he didn't start taking the law into his own hands.

Luke couldn't begin to think how he'd react under those circumstances, but he thought he'd stick to the law. He may not be the best sheriff — but he was the only one and he was charged with protecting the community as best he could. Right now, he thought, maybe his best wasn't good enough.

The trail veered to the left and the Meadows' house came into view. Neat, tidy, well-run, the ashes of the barn being blown along the ground by the breeze made him realize how quickly things could change.

Luke tethered his horse at the hitching rail at the foot of the steps that led up to the small verandah. Strange, he thought, no sign of activity. Then he reckoned they'd still be out in the fields gathering in the harvest, or maybe working on some other farm. He climbed the steps and knocked on the door.

Luke waited a few moments, but his knocking elicited no response. He walked round the back of the house, making sure Jessie wasn't busy in the kitchen and, peering through the window, he saw that it was empty.

The sound of a galloping horse made him draw his gun and his pulse quickened. Keeping close to the building, he skirted back to the front of the house. In the distance he saw the rider, there was something familiar about him, but Luke kept hidden until he could see the man clearly.

Arnie Dillon rode straight up to Luke's parked horse and dismounted. The sheriff reholstered his weapon and walked to the front steps.

"Arnie, how're you doin'?" Luke asked.

"Howdy, Luke. I'm fine, jus' rode on out to see where Hank and Jessie are. They were due over to my place 'bout noon, but they ain't showed up. It ain't like 'em."

"Well, they ain't here. Is there another farm they could be at?"

"Nope. We got a system out here. Everyone knows where to be come harvest. Hell, it was Hank that dreamed it up in the first place." Arnie took his Stetson off and dried the inside band with his bandanna.

"I didn't pass 'em on the way out an' they sure weren't in town," Luke said.

"Then where the hell they gone?" Arnie asked, scanning the horizon.

"I don't know, but I'm gonna take a ride round their place and then double check on Caleb's place, see if'n they're there."

"Okay, Luke. Look, I'd like to ride

with you but, well, I gotta get my crop in an' . . . "

"Don't worry none, Arnie. If'n I find 'em I'll ride on over an' let you know." Luke climbed into his saddle. "You get back to your place an' I'll catch you later."

Caleb's place had seemed deserted as he rode through earlier, but he wasn't really looking for anything there, he was more intent on seeing Hank and Jessie.

Arnie rode back to his own fields and Luke set off at a canter. Although he'd not said so, he was getting a mite worried about the whereabouts of Hank and Jessie.

* * *

Despite his intended vigilance, Hank was unused to just sitting doing nothing.

He kept watch over the prairie valley for four hours now and boredom was setting in to the extent he could hardly keep his eyes open. He'd stood and walked round for a while, drunk water from his canteen and splashed some on his face, but to no avail. He was plain tuckered out with waiting.

The heat from both sun and the reflected heat rising off the rocks was making him so drowsy and sweaty that he felt he had no alternative other than to take a nap. He took a last sweeping glance round the prairie, watched as small figures toiled endlessly in a corn field and felt a smack of guilt: he should be down there with them, lending a hand as they had him. But it was too late now. The anger he felt in the pit of his stomach and the vengeance that filled his head was too much.

Hank reasoned his weakness out: there wasn't likely to be an attack while men were out toiling, they'd wait — if they ever showed up again — until all was quiet so if he was to stay awake all night, now was the best time to grab some shut-eye.

Made sense to him.

Moving his saddle and arranging his bedroll, Hank sunk gratefully to the ground. Inside two minutes, he was asleep.

* * *

The first of the whiskey bottles had been drunk as the three men rode out to their campsite at the creek.

"Hell, boys, could life git better?" King shouted as they cantered along the trail.

"Shit, man this is the best," Weaver agreed taking a swig from the second bottle.

"Better yet to grab a piece o' that woman's ass, *that*'s the best," Masters added.

Ahead, the creek swung into view and with it their campsite hidden among the rocks.

"Shit, the buckboard's gone," King said reining in his horse.

"Let's see if there's any tracks we kin

follow, she can't've got far." Weaver sped his horse on to the old ford.

They stopped in the middle of the creek, surveying the surrounding countryside.

"Hell, she could be back in town by now," Kid Weaver said.

"I doubt that," King answered. "There's only one trail to Liberty an' we jus' rode out on it."

"Goddamn, you're right. She must've veered off the trail," Masters said

"Good thinking," King said sarcastically. "Come on, let's go take a look-see."

The three wheeled their animals and walked across the ford to the far bank where the rock turned to sand before the grass started to grow.

"Got 'em." It was Kid Weaver who spotted the wheel tracks first. "Look, they head on down back the trail."

"Well, let's git goin'," King said and dug his heels into the flanks of his horse.

The trail left by the buckboard was

easy to follow; if the three men had been paying more attention on the way out, they'd have spotted them earlier and maybe saved themselves some time.

The whiskey and the heat was beginning to have an effect on all three men, to the extent that, although they never said as much to each other, they felt more like sleeping than humping.

Having ridden for only twenty minutes they soon came across the abandoned buckboard and then had a choice of two sets of tracks to follow.

"Shit!" King said as he wiped the sweat from his face with both hands. "Which way now?" He looked at the two sets of tracks which headed off in a V formation.

"Reckon she'll try gettin' to town," Weaver said.

"I ain't ridin' in that way agen," Masters added. "I'm plumb tuckered out."

"I know where she lives," King

said. "Mebbe we could go give her a visit tonight?" He grinned at his two partners.

"Sure beats ridin' round in this heat," Weaver said.

"I'm game, only let's decide one way or the other," Masters said, his patience running thin.

"Come on, let's head back to the creek. We got some work on tonight, an' then . . . " He was still grinning as they set off.

★ ★ ★

Luke reached Caleb's house to find it deserted. He walked across to the barn — nothing. The place was empty. Didn't look as if anyone had been near the place for weeks, but he knew that couldn't be true.

He was about to ride on when he heard the sound of a rider approaching; leaving the barn, he walked out into the compound in time to see the fancy buggy of Bart Honer draw up.

"Howdy, Mr Honer," Luke called out.

Honer nearly jumped out of his skin.

"Sheriff. What brings you out here?" Honer asked.

"I was about to ask you the same thing, Mr Honer."

"I own the place," Honer replied, stepping down off the buggy. "Bought it out this morning."

"Is that a fact?" Luke said.

"Sure is. The mortgage was in arrears and Mr Moss owed more to the bank than the property was worth."

"Is that a fact?" Luke said again.

"You think I'm lying, Sheriff?"

"Hell, no. Jus' didn't figure you a farmer, is all."

"*I'm* not a farmer, Sheriff. But you don't have to be to own a parcel of land."

"You're sure right there, Mr Honer."

"Besides, can't work at the bank forever," Honer added.

"That's a fact," Luke said. "Trouble

is now," he went on, "town's paid fer the funeral, an' it don't look like there's anything comin' from this place."

"I'd be happy to pay for that, Sheriff. Least I can do."

"That's mighty neighbourly of you Mr Honer. Mighty neighbourly."

"My pleasure, Sheriff. Now, if you'll excuse me, I need to take stock."

"Yeah, sure, I was leavin' anyways. See you around, Mr Honer."

"Sheriff."

Luke mounted up and watched as Honer entered the house. What the hell does he want with old man Moss's place? Luke thought. He stored that thought away and headed out towards the creek through Moss's field and on across Arnie Dillon's land.

The sun was beginning to set, but the heat rising up from the land was intense, stifling almost. Luke looked forward to the cooler night air. Already, he saw the faint outline of the moon, looking like a ghostly face in the sky as he neared the creek.

His horse sniffed at the breeze, picking up the scent of the water and, without Luke doing anything, the horse broke out of the steady trot and into a canter towards the creek.

He saw the three riders before he heard them. Pulling up in the shade of a tree, Luke watched as the three men rode on past the ford and up towards the outcrop.

Now who the hell are they? he thought. Better check 'em out I guess.

Leading his horse to the creek, Luke let the animal drink its fill. He took his Stetson off and filled it with water, then poured it over his head. The shock of the cold water felt good, real good.

Mounting up, he walked the horse towards the outcrop, his right hand resting, automatically, on the butt of his Colt.

"Howdy boys," Luke said as he entered the hollow.

The three men, weary with heat and whiskey, were taken by surprise.

King was the first to react. He saw the tin star and was immediately on his guard. Weaver and Masters rose drowsily. Although they'd just arrived, all three had fallen more or less straight asleep.

"Help you, Sheriff?" King said.

"Maybe. Maybe not. You boys plannin' on stayin' around long?" Luke asked.

"As you said, Sheriff. Maybe, maybe not. Depends on the work."

Luke looked at the three men. Fully loaded, low slung gunbelts, caught his attention as did the cold black eyes of the man who'd spoken.

"You boys don't look like farm hands to me," Luke said.

"Well, these days man's gotta take what he can find, Sheriff," King said.

"Seen anyone on your travels?" Luke asked.

"Plenty, Sheriff," Master spoke up now. "Anyone in particular?"

"Man and a woman."

"Hell, we seen plenty o' them,"

Weaver said, a grin spreading across his stubbled face.

"Recently," Luke said bluntly. "Not since we left town."

"When was that?"

"'Bout an hour ago."

"I jus' saw you come in," Luke said. "Town's only thirty-minutes down the trail."

"Maybe it was thirty-minutes, then," King said. "Didn't keep a check on the time. Didn't think I had to."

The three men had by now adopted the position. Feet placed about eighteen inches apart, arms hanging deceptively loose by their sides. They stood about four feet apart and Luke felt a cold shiver run down his back.

There was no way, he knew, he could take on all three. And he got the definite impression that, if he said the wrong word, his life wouldn't be worth a spit.

"Well," he went on, trying to keep his voice cool and authoritative, "if you do come across two folks, be obliged if'n you'd let me know. I'll be seein' you."

Luke wheeled his horse round and walked it slowly out of the hollow. Every muscle in his body tensed.

"Yeah, be seein' you, too, Sheriff," a voice rang out behind him.

"Sure as shit," another voice said.

Luke continued to walk his animal away from the three men. The sweat running freely down his face and neck and back. He reached the end of the hollow, just where the creek ran past, when the shot was fired.

8

JESSIE MEADOWS opened her eyes. The sky was a deep purple and she could no longer feel the heat of the sun on her face.

She must have been out for a couple of hours at least, she thought. Her tongue felt strange, thick and dry, it seemed to fill her mouth. Her head was still throbbing, but nowhere near as badly as earlier in the day.

She sat up her head swimming, but, focusing on a bush, she saw only the one. Her eyesight was at least back to normal.

She turned her head, sending a fresh wave of throbbing which seemed as if it were about to burst her eyeballs. She scanned her surroundings: no sign of the horse.

Memory flooded back, the knock on the head, the ropes, the buckboard, the

115

ground rushing up to meet her — then oblivion.

She was heading to town to see the sheriff. Where was Hank? What was he doing?

She stood slowly, raising herself up on her arms first, then onto her feet. Swaying slightly, trying to lick dry lips with a dry tongue, she set off. She'd only gone a few yards when she realized she had no idea of which direction to go.

She looked up at the early evening sky, then across to the distant horizon. Her brain wouldn't function. Did the sun rise in the east or the west? Where did it set? She couldn't think straight. Still swaying, she put her hands to her face, as if that action might make her brain function, and for the first time that day, tears rolled gently down her cheeks.

Pulling herself together, she gritted her teeth in an attempt to stop the sobs that hovered just below the surface from breaking out. She breathed in hard and long, feeling the cool air fill her lungs. She breathed out through her mouth, the back of her throat burning as she did so.

Steadying herself, her brain clicked in to working again. Rises in the east, sets in the west. The west, stupid, she chided herself.

Once again, she looked towards the distant horizon, searching for the faint, red glow that would give her directions. For an instant, she regretted not listening more closely to Hank as he pointed stars out to her, but at those moments of love, the stars were an added romantic bonus, rather than a life-saving entity.

She caught the last of what she thought to be a dull-red glow and fixed her eyes on a tree that was more or less in line. West, she thought. The town lies east. Keeping the tree visible, its black shape looking rather like a bee-hive, she slowly turned and fixed on another tree. East.

Jessie Meadows set off for town.

★ ★ ★

Hank awoke with a start. Shivering slightly, he was annoyed with himself for sleeping far longer than he'd planned. He rubbed the sleep out of his eyes and stood, stretching as he did so. These rocks sure are hard, he thought, rubbing at his backside in an attempt to get the circulation going.

The valley floor spread out before him in varying shades of blackness. In the far distance, twinkling lights shone at the far end of the prairie. Liberty, he thought.

Close in, smaller lights showed up now and then, as if someone were turning an oil-lamp on and off, but Hank realized a tree or bush was probably swaying in the cool night air.

From behind and above, Hank heard the baying of distant coyotes, about to begin their nightly search for food. Crickets added to the sounds drifting in and out of the night breeze, along with noises that he just couldn't explain.

His horse, patient as ever, was still picking at the sparse vegetation and Hank took down the canteen and washed his mouth out before taking a drink of the warm water inside.

Feeling more refreshed, but still thirsty, he scanned the prairie and farmlands again.

In the blackness, he thought several times he'd seen moving objects: black shadows darting in and out of cover, running across the top of the corn stubble. But every time he tried to focus on the fleeting objects, they disappeared.

Rubbing his eyes again, he tried once more to catch sight of any moving object, but as he caught movement out of the corner of his eye he looked at where he thought it was, and it had gone.

In several parts of the valley, a mist began to rise as the heat of the land evaporated into the colder night air. Spectral shapes formed, illuminated by the eery light of the moon, only to disappear as the breeze whisked them away. Hank decided keeping a watch out at night was going to be a difficult task.

* * *

The slug smashed into Luke Garrett's back, slamming him face down on the neck of his horse. Instinct made him keep hold of the reins and his last conscious effort was wrapping the strip of leather tightly round his wrist.

The blast from the hand-gun had sent his horse galloping forward in a state of panic, straight out of the hollow, across the ford and down the trail to Liberty. Luke hung on, barely conscious, all he wanted to do was close his eyes. But he didn't. He knew that if he did, he might never open them again.

King watched the slug hit the sheriff and gave the man very little chance of surviving. He already knew there was no proper doctor in Liberty and that if the bullet hadn't ripped his insides apart, infection sure would finish him off.

"Let's git after him!" Weaver yelled.

"Naw, no point. I seen dead men afore," King said, reholstering his gun. "An' that's another I seen jus' riding out. If'n he makes it to town, it'll be as a corpse."

"I still reckon we git him," Weaver said.

"There ain't no one in town who's gonna do a dang thing. Relax, git the coffee on, we got ourselves a busy night. I reckon the sun'll go down in less than an hour. Most folks will be home, eatin'. That's when we hit."

Weaver wasn't convinced, but he knew better than to go against King. He busied himself setting the coffee pot on the fire, but he couldn't get rid of his bad feelings.

King, meanwhile, merely loaded in another slug into the barrel of his

Colt to replace the one he'd fired. He aimed to be ready at all times. No point thinking you had six slugs and only having five. Men died that way, but not Dirk King.

Carefully, almost lovingly, he loaded his quiver with the arrows he'd prepared. He just hoped the oil would burn as well as the pitch.

Weaver poured out the coffee and the three men sat and drank the scalding brew, waiting for the night to come down.

★ ★ ★

Luke Garrett felt waves of pain shoot through his back at each bounce of the saddle. The reins had began to cut off the circulation to his left hand where he'd tied the leather too tight. He ignored that pain, and gritted his teeth. He had to get to town — fast.

Luke wasn't sure how badly he'd been injured. He could move his arms and legs, but his neck hurt either with the jolting or from the effect of the bullet.

Either way, Luke knew that if he didn't make town, he was a gonner.

The horse began to slow, the panic gone and, without proper direction from his passenger, it more or less made up its own mind on what pace to travel at.

As it slowed, so the jolting became less severe, and Luke was thankful for that.

The sun began to set and darkness descended across the prairie. In that eery time before the sun finally disappeared and the moon took over, eyesight played funny tricks on a man, even a fit man.

The watery, yellow light had an unreal quality about it, like when you first open your eyes in the morning in a darkened room. Only instead of waking, Luke began to drift off into an interrupted sleep. His eyes closed for only seconds before he'd snap them open again, but those seconds felt like minutes and Luke knew he was drifting.

A sweat broke out over his entire body and, whether because the sun was losing its heat, or the bullet in his back, Luke began to shiver. It seemed all his body heat was escaping through the hole in his back.

He dug his heels into the flanks of his horse and a fresh wave of pain seared through his body making him yell out in agony. The horse cantered, as instructed.

Luke began to see the grass in minute detail, he even thought he could see the bugs crawling all over it, and when he saw the woman, he wasn't surprised at all. He knew it was a figment of his imagination.

He blinked rapidly, trying to clear his head, then his ears started playing up on him as well when he heard the woman call out his name.

"Luke! Luke, is that you?"

Smiling to himself, even though in great pain, Luke Garrett ignored the call. Convinced as he was that it was all part of a waking dream.

"Luke! it's me, Jessie, Jessie Meadows!"

Still Luke ignored the sound of the voice; he figured as he'd been looking for Hank and Jessie, his brain had that one thought in mind and was manifesting it now.

"Luke! Stop!"

Luke felt the reins being tugged and through pain-racked eyes he saw the face of Jessie Meadows staring up at him. He pulled as hard as he could on the reins and his mount came to a halt. Luke slumped forwards, his battle to stay awake was lost.

★ ★ ★

Night fell. The hollow, surrounded as it was with high rocks, was a bowl of blackness, lit only by the small campfire, which Dirk King doused with the dregs of his coffee mug.

The three men mounted up and walked their animals out onto the prairie where the moon gave them more than enough light to ride by.

The effects of the whiskey had long since disappeared and, sober, they headed for the next target that King had already decided to hit: the farm of Arnie Dillon.

The three rode in silence, for Weaver and Masters it was their first excursion, so they were a touch apprehensive. With King carrying the means for destruction, they figured they were only there to make up the numbers.

The ride out to Dillon's place would take an hour, they were in no rush. King knew that dirtfarmers ate when the sun went down and slept through the night until at least an hour before sunrise, so they could maximize daylight hours.

To King's mind, a stupid and pointless existence.

"'Sposin' someone sees us?" Weaver asked.

"Then it'll be the *last* thing they see," King laughed as he said it.

"I still don't figure what we're gonna

do with a farm," Master said.

"What we're gonna do is *employ* people to run it," King said. "'Cept I don't aim to run no dirtfarm. I reckon this whole valley will become a single ranch, and, boys, we will be running the best beef steers around. That's where the money is these days: cattle."

"I don't know the first thing about cattle, 'ceptin' maybe brandin'," Weaver said.

"Don't make no difference. How hard can it be? There's already some cows out there an' there's enough grass to feed 'em. All we gotta do is sell 'em," King said.

"What about Honer? He part o' this grand plan o' yours?" Masters asked.

"Hell, no. That fat pig ain't gonna see the month out. Soon's all the bank figurin' is done and the deeds is ours, he'll be long gone." King laughed again, a laugh that worried Weaver and Masters.

9

THE town was deathly quiet as the sun finally gave up the daylight hours and night-time took over.

Oil lamps twinkled through dust coated windows, or from behind thin cotton drapes and shed small pools of light across the empty boardwalks. Silence reigned, the only sound coming from the wind as it forced its way around the man-made structures, rattling a loose board here, a swinging sign there.

Apart from Samuel K. Vermont and Deke Wilmot, even the saloon was empty, an unusual phenomena at any time of the day but particularly so now.

It was as if Liberty was waiting for something to happen: something it was afraid of.

The buildings themselves seemed to close in on Main and Elm, huddling together for protection and safety.

Sam and Deke drank whiskey, silently, not really enjoying the experience but it was something they did together most early evenings.

"I don't like the feel o' things." Deke spoke first.

"Feels like there's a storm a-brewin', 'cept, there ain't," Sam said.

"Not of the weather variety, anyways," Deke added.

"Folks can feel it," Sam said bringing the whiskey bottle out from under the counter. It was their bottle, not the cheap, domestic rot-gut, but a bottle Sam had bought from a carpet-bagger who'd lost his way and finished up in Liberty. The rampant stag on the label and the slogan: 'Produce of Scotland' had been all he needed to know. That, and the fact that the cork hadn't been tampered with.

Carefully, he poured out two more small measures. Both men reckoned, at this rate, the bottle would last another two weeks — if they were careful, then it was back to the rot-gut.

"Man don't have too many pleasures," Deke said pensively. "But this sure is one of 'em." He lifted the small glass up to eye-level and peered through the light amber liquid. "See that, clear as a bell," he added.

"One-hundred per cent," Sam said. They clinked glasses in a silent toast and downed their final drink for the night.

"Thanks, Sam. I'll be taking my leave now. Think I'll check up on my medical bag, never know when I'll be needin' it."

"Let's hope you won't be needin' it tonight," Sam said.

"Let's hope," Deke agreed and he left the saloon. The balmy night air, in contrast to the heat of the day, felt cool and refreshing as the wind blew into Deke's face. He removed his battered Stetson, feeling the wind tussle at what hair he had left. Breathing in deeply, he tasted the air, mixed with the small amount of whiskey he'd consumed, and all seemed right with the world. Except it didn't. He couldn't rid himself of the thought of impending doom, hence his eagerness to ensure his black bag was stocked up with bandages, thread, needles, quinine, alcohol, and anything else he could think of.

Deke walked down a deserted Main Street towards his own place and a shiver ran down his spine.

★ ★ ★

Luke Garrett managed to stay in the saddle, his eyelids fluttering like the wings on a hovering butterfly, in an attempt to stay conscious. Jessie, at first unaware of his wound had talked ten to the dozen as she reached for his canteen and splashed water on her face before rinsing her mouth out and taking a few tentative sips of the luke-warm water.

Luke was in no condition to hold a

conversation, that was obvious to her. Sweat was running down his face and his shirt was soaked through. She was grateful for the fact that he'd managed to stay in the saddle for there was no way she could have lifted him.

Carefully, she adjusted Luke's body-weight so that he leaned over slightly to the left. His left foot taking most of his weight, she slid his right foot out of the stirrup.

Hitching up her dress, she placed her right foot in the vacant saddle and, holding the pommel with her right hand and Luke's arm with her left, she jumped up, swung her left leg over behind the saddle and grabbed the reins at the same time from behind Luke.

Luke's body rested mainly on her left arm and, at least for the time being, she could take the strain. There was no way she could get his right foot back in the stirrup.

Digging her booted feet into the horse's side, she set off for Liberty, praying Luke would stay atop the horse.

The horse bore the extra weight effortlessly and Jessie, a horsewoman of some repute, kept the animal at a steady trot.

After ten minutes, she saw way ahead a small light. It was quickly joined by two or three others: Liberty.

Breathing a sigh of relief that she and Luke would make it, her thoughts and fears now turned to how badly Luke was injured, something she hadn't even thought about.

Keeping her eyes pinned firmly on the twinkling lights, Jessie urged the animal on. Safety was only a few hundred yards away now and she prayed once again that Deke was both at home *and* sober.

Reining in outside Deke's house she saw the lights on in his surgery and also the bulky figure of Deke as he crossed past the window. Jessie now had a problem: how to dismount without letting Luke fall to the ground and

133

injuring himself further?

She stayed atop the horse and yelled and screamed louder than she thought possible.

Inside the house, Deke nearly jumped out of his skin. The bottle of quinine he was holding fell to the floor, luckily onto a carpet and not bare floorboards.

Pulling back the drapes, he peered through the window, but the light from the house wasn't bright enough to see who the hell was screaming and shouting like a banshee.

Taking out his gun, Deke made for the front door. He cocked the hammer and, taking a deep breath, opened the door and quickly stepped out onto the small verandah.

"Jessie?" Deke said. "What the hell's happened?"

"Deke, I don't know. I think Luke's been shot but I don't know where an' I can't get down without him falling."

Deke released the hammer on his handgun and reholstered it. He ran across the verandah and down the steps to the side of the horse.

"If you can put Luke's foot back in the stirrup and pull him towards you, I can dismount and give you a hand to get him down."

By this time, Luke was delirious. Mumbling and muttering to himself incoherently, and Deke knew he was in no position to help himself dismount.

Doing as he was asked, Jessie jumped to the ground and between them, they lowered Luke off the saddle.

"You take his legs," Deke ordered.

Jessie could smell alcohol on Deke's breath as he spoke to her, but the old man's voice was strong and firm. She did as Deke ordered and they carried him through the house and laid Luke on the leather-covered table that Deke operated on man and beast alike.

"Jesus!" Deke said. "Have you seen your dress?"

Jessie looked down at the blood-stain that ran from her neck to her waist without saying a word.

Deke looked her in the eyes, then he noticed the dried blood at the side of her neck.

"What the hell's goin' on here?" he asked.

"I'll tell you later, Deke," Jessie said.

Deke Wilmot knew enough not to question her further. Already he could see signs of shock appearing on Jessie's face. Without further ado, he shifted his attention back to the now silent and unconscious Luke Garrett.

He checked his chest and legs, but they were free of injury. "Jessie, help me roll him onto his stomach."

Jessie stood where she was, her eyes as wide as a plate of eggs.

"Jessie? Can you hear me?" Deke shouted.

Still Jessie didn't move.

Ignoring her for the present, Deke man-handled Luke onto his stomach. The site of the wound was obvious as he stared at Luke's blood-soaked shirt.

"Jesus, Mary an' Joseph," Deke said

to himself. "He's bin danged shot in the back!"

Grabbing a pair of scissors, Deke quickly removed Luke's shirt. The bullet wound was high up to the right of the spine and just below the shoulder-blade. Well, Deke thought, at least if you're gonna be shot in the back, that's the best place to get it.

There was no exit wound, so Deke knew the slug was still in there. He also knew it had to come out and he was thankful that Luke was way out of it.

He quickly washed his hands in soap and water, then poured alcohol over them, before pouring the contents of the small bottle into Luke's wound.

Luke, although unconscious, moved visibly as the stinging liquid burned into the gaping hole.

Without wasting any time, Deke doused a scalpel with more alcohol and made two incisions across the entry wound, forming a cross. He peeled the tissue back and, using a probe, he gently and carefully prodded into the hole he'd enlarged.

Out of the corner of his eye, he saw Jessie sink gracefully into a leather chair, her head leaning to one side. She'd either fainted, he thought, or she's just plumb tuckered out. But he didn't dwell on her for too long.

By the light of two oil-lamps, not in any way bright enough, Deke probed and prodded. Sometimes hitting bone, sometimes muscle; then he hit lead.

He grabbed a small pair of forceps and, keeping the probe resting on what he hoped to hell was the bullet he had to remove, he inserted the forceps without even trying to sterilize them, and made a lunge for the slug.

Twice he thought he'd got it, only for the forceps to snap shut and lock on themselves, which meant retracting them and releasing the locking mechanism. Third time, he struck lucky, the forceps clamped round the bullet and he slowly, carefully, began to pull.

Dismounting, Dirk King pulled the quiver and bow from his back and, as was his custom, lit a cheroot, tossing the match to the ground.

Kid Weaver and Brent Masters sat atop their horses and gazed ahead at the small shack and barn that was their first target. The tidy homestead of Arnie Dillon showed no lights, just as King had anticipated.

"See, these shit-head dirtfarmers spend most o' their time asleep," he said, not trying to keep his voice down.

"Let's git this over with," Weaver said. He wasn't feeling particularly nervous, merely exposed. There was no cover and, for a fleeting moment, he'd envisaged an ambush. He saw all the dirtfarmers just a-lying in wait, waiting for them to strike again, and it sent a shiver down his spine.

Leisurely, King finished his cheroot and flicked it to the ground. He removed one arrow, sighted down it, again, as was his custom. He already knew that each and every arrow was as straight and even as they could be.

"Come on over here," he said to his two partners.

They dismounted and walked across the ground towards him. King took out two more arrows and handed one to each.

"Now, when I say, set fire to the wadding, but not until I say so. Got it?"

Both men nodded.

King grinned as he slowly took out a match and struck it in his gunbelt. He ignited the wadding and set the arrow to bow. Sighting down the shaft, he pulled the bow taut and loosed off the flaming arrow.

All three watched as it arced through the night sky and thudded, unceremoniously, onto the front door of the shack. Instantly, the dry timber caught fire and, within seconds, the flames were licking at the roof.

"Now!" King shouted to Weaver.

Weaver struck a match and handed the arrow to King. He loosed it off and this time, the arrow landed on the small, corn-filled barn; that too burst into flame.

"An' agen!" he turned his attention to Master, who followed suit and handed the flaming arrow to King.

King waited a few seconds this time. Shifting his gaze from shack to barn, trying to decide which of the two needed extra help. He decided on the shack.

For the third time, a flaming arrow sailed through the sky and thudded onto the roof of the already burning shack.

"That should do it," he said casually, more to himself than anyone else.

The three men stood and watched as the dancing orange and red flames danced their way higher into the night sky, sending up a plume of sparks as they did so.

Even from this distance, they could feel the heat of the fire. King, a grin on his face, watched as part of the shack roof collapsed inwards, sending an even greater plume of sparks and smoke into the air.

Still grinning as the front door — the only door — burst open. A man, at least they could only assume it was a man, stumbled from the blazing building.

A sheet of flame engulfed him as he blindly groped his way out of the building where he stood for what seemed like hours, a living, human torch, before he slowly and soundlessly crumpled to the ground.

* * *

Hank Meadows could hardly believe his eyes. The signs he'd been waiting for had appeared and yet he stood transfixed, unable to move, as he saw one, two, three flaming objects sail through the air like comets, before landing again.

Then he watched as the flames,

small and indistinct at first, started to grow. He was fascinated: it wasn't the reaction he'd intended or planned for. His hopes of a rescue, riding through the night and saving man and property, now seemed futile as he watched the two separate fires grow and grow and grow.

As if hypnotized, he watched, rather like a child watching a burning stove, as the flames danced higher into the air.

"Jesus!" he muttered, almost in awe. "Arnie. Arnie Dillon!"

His own voice seemed to break the trance he was in and he was immediately galvanized into action. Saddling up, wishing he hadn't taken the saddle off in the first place as he wasted even more time, Hank mounted and, although he wanted to gallop, he had to slowly walk the horse down the path between the rocks before he hit the level ground.

"I'm comin', Arnie," he said softly. "I'm comin'!"

10

BREATHING evenly, Deke Wilmot began the arduous task of removing the slug from Luke's back. Slowly, slowly, he said to himself. He was waiting for any signs of an artery being hit, dislodging the bullet could cause more harm than leaving it in.

Sweat was pouring from Deke's face. Normally, he'd have Wash or even Sam standing by, but there was no time to get them and, with Jessie out cold, he was on his own.

Keeping his old, gnarled hands as steady as he could he heard the slight sucking sound as the bullet was pulled from the tissue it was embedded in.

Luke groaned. Deke hadn't time to get him drunk, or knock him out and the ether was still in his bag. Deke just hoped Luke didn't regain consciousness just yet.

"Goddamn!" he said out loud, "why the hell ain't I got more light!"

The flickering oil-lamps did their best, but the shadows created by Deke's arms and the wound itself, prevented him from seeing as much as he knew he should.

Slowly, he raised the forceps. He looked down the iron shaft, trying to gauge how much was left inside: he reckoned two inches.

Deke took a lungful of warm air and continued to extract the forceps. Painfully slow, he couldn't rush. A small bubble of blood rose to the surface and Deke froze.

Had he caught something with either the forceps or had the dislodged bullet been resting near a vein? He couldn't tell, but the blood wasn't spurting, it was just a gentle trickle. He continued to pull.

Deke saw the clamp of the forceps appear, blood-smeared, and then to the slug. The bleeding didn't get any worse, thank God.

The forceps came clear, and with it the bullet, free at last.

Dropping both into a bowl, Deke grabbed some cotton wadding and began dabbing hard at the gaping wound. He kept pressure on the hole and then slowly released the blood-soaked cloth and, lifting one of the oil-lamps now that he had a spare hand, he peered over the top of his eye-glasses.

Luke had been lucky. So had Deke, he thought. Only a tiny pool of blood appeared in the wound and Deke knew he could handle that.

He placed the oil-lamp back on the table and, with the relief of removing the slug without causing Luke any more grief, his hands began to shake a little as he relaxed.

He mopped his own brow, and then tried to thread a needle so he could close the muscle tissue and then the skin.

Peering through his eye-glasses, tongue licking his dry lips, Deke tried four times before he managed to thread the needle. Now, he thought, Luke, you stay still while I stitch you up good and proper.

Inserting the needle, he drew the two bloody lumps of muscle together and sewed them up, then, he did the same with the skin. The stitches inside would take care of themselves eventually, but the outside ones would need to be removed.

Grabbing bandages and wadding, Deke bound up Luke's chest and back tightly; the pressure of the wadding would cut the risk of internal bleeding down, and, as long as Luke rested up a while, he should pull through — or at least — Deke hoped he would.

Deke left Luke lying face down and then turned his attention to Jessie: She was still out cold and Deke turned her head to one side.

"Well, little lady, I don't know what you bin up to, but you're sure gonna have a headache come mornin'," he said as he inspected the lump on her forehead and the dark-blue bruise that had already started to appear on the back of her neck.

Using the rubbing-alcohol again, Deke cleaned up the grazed forehead and wiped Jessie's neck clean. He cut off some cloth and, using plaster, he stuck it over the graze on her forehead. There was no point in putting anything on her neck, Mother Nature would take care of that.

Pulling a wooden stool closer to the chair, Deke lifted Jessie's feet and placed them on it.

"Sleep, little lady, best medicine there is."

Checking out Luke and satisfied he was as well as could be expected, Deke slumped into the other armchair and, within seconds, his snores filled the small room.

★ ★ ★

Bart Honer had been through Caleb Moss's shack with a fine tooth-comb, he'd also checked out the lean-to out back, but had come up with nothing valuable.

Not that he'd really expected to, but he'd heard tales of some of these hick-farmers stashing money or collecting fine things that you wouldn't expect.

But not Caleb Moss.

The shack was furnished, if you could call it that, with a table, and two chairs that looked as if Caleb had hewn them himself. There was a small cot, a wood-stove, a chest of drawers and a wash-bowl and pitcher. And that was it.

Honer walked over to the barn. There was a mangy horse stabled there, although with all the things you'd expect to find on a small farm, but nothing of any value.

Honer had already decided that the whole lot would be razed to the ground as soon as he'd acquired the Meadows' place, and then he could begin to build the sort of house that would befit a man of his position: the largest land-owner and rancher in the county.

In his mind's eye, he saw himself surrounded by all the luxury money and power would bring: champagne, a drink he'd only heard of but never seen or tasted, crystal, gold, women. He was getting sexually excited at the thought of it all, and the thought of Jessie Meadows.

He began to wonder how he could broach the subject of killing Hank Meadows to Dirk King. Surely the man would have no qualms, after all, he'd killed before, he'd already told him as much and, having killed once . . .

Yes, Honer thought, King would do it and Honer would be Jessie Meadows' saviour. She'd learn to love him, his money and his power until, that is, he got tired of her.

But that was a long way off. Night was coming fast and Honer didn't want to be out on the trail in the dark — not after his last trip home from the hoe-down. This place wasn't safe yet. Maybe I should get a few good men around me, he thought. Yes, my own private army.

The light began to fail and as Honer was about to leave, he noticed the small trap-door set in the floor. A sack was covering most of it and the table was atop it but he had to take a look at whatever was underneath.

Shifting the heavy wooden table to one side, Honer kicked the sacking out the way and exposed the sand covered trap-door. There was a rough metal ring at one end and Honer inserted a finger into it and pulled. The door was too heavy to lift with just one finger, so he grabbed the metal ring with both hands and yanked it up.

Beneath his feet was a black hole it was impossible to see into. Honer looked round for a lamp. He saw one hanging on a nail above the wash-bowl, all he needed now was a match. He felt his vest pockets but, as he only ever had a cigar in the office, he had no matches on him.

Surely, he thought, Moss must have kept some somewhere? He began to search once more and found them in a glass jar in the chest of drawers. He struck a match and lit the lamp.

Black smoke poured from the glass top, the wick obviously not trimmed properly. Honer tutted. In his book, a man who couldn't be bothered to trim his wick wasn't worth his salt.

Holding the lamp high in the failing darkness, Honer peered into the abyss. Still, he could make no definition. He had no alternative other than to climb down the stairs for a better look.

Placing the lamp on the floor, Honer backed down the rickety steps, picking up the lamp as his head reached floor level.

The cellar, rough hewn and unlined, was just a tad smaller than the room upstairs, and it was empty. Honer cursed. What a waste of time and energy that had proved to be.

He was about to climb out of the cellar when he heard a thud on the roof. Within seconds, the floor above was filled with white, cloying smoke.

"Jesus! No!" he shouted.

But no one heard him.

★ ★ ★

By the time Hank made it across the prairie riding rough-shod through fields of unharvested corn, all that was left of Arnie Dillon's place was glowing embers.

Outside, where the front door had been, Hank saw the charred remains of what he supposed was once a human being. Now, it was a blackened lump of meat. The hands and most of the arms were reduced to ashes that would quickly be dispersed by the wind. The feet, too, had burned right through leaving stumps of legs. The flesh on the exposed face had burned through to the bone, exposing gums and teeth in a terrible grimace.

Hank turned away from Arnie's body and threw up 'til he could throw up no more. He tasted bile and spat into the dirt.

Turning, he made a solemn, silent promise to his old friend.

There was nothing Hank could do now. Down the trail he heard the sound of rolling wheels: it didn't take long for folks to rally round, they were getting used to it by now.

Hank didn't wait for the men to arrive. He needed to find whoever had fired Arnie's place and he'd lost too much time as it was.

From his lofty position, he had ascertained the direction in which the burning arrows — for that, he reasoned, was surely what they must have been — had been fired.

So, assuming the bowman, or men, had ridden off in the opposite direction, Hank knew where to start his search.

He dug his heels into the horse's side and set off at a gallop. From behind, he heard shots. Hell, he thought, they think I'm the one who started the fire.

Hank rode on, keeping his head low and pretty soon he was out of shot. He hit the trail that led on to the old ford and reined in his animal. Dismounting, he peered through the moon-lit night at the trail itself and slowly walked forwards. After twenty feet or so, he found a set of boot prints, fresh, and a burned out cheroot. To the side of these prints, he saw two more sets of prints and one of them had a broken heel that was plainly visible even to the untrained eye.

He followed the tracks which ended where the men, for now he knew there were at least three, had mounted up. He saw in the failing light, just before a dark cloud passed across the face of the moon, that the horses had left going east — not west as he would have anticipated.

East? What the hell, there was only Caleb's place and . . . Shit an' hellfire, his place!

Hank remounted and set off at a gallop. It would only take five, ten minutes to get there, assuming the men intended to fire that place too.

As he rode, he kept his eyes trained ahead, peering into the now inky blackness, looking for he knew not what. Except as he looked he saw the tell-tale trail of flame arc through the sky once more and, within minutes, white smoke and flames appeared.

Once again, Hank was too late, but this time, he was only minutes away from the men who'd killed two of his friends. This time they wouldn't get away so easily.

* * *

A loud groan and instantly, Deke Wilmot snapped open his eyes. There, sitting up on the table, was Luke Garrett, head bowed and wincing.

"What the hell d'you think you're doin'?" Deke shouted.

The old man jumped up far quicker than he should have been able to, and caught Luke just as he was about to fall to the floor.

Carefully, Deke lowered the sheriff

156

back onto the table.

"Dang fool," he muttered, "don't you know you bin shot up pretty damn bad?"

Luke opened his eyes and stared up at Deke. For a moment, there was no recognition, then a slow grin spread across Luke's face. He coughed. Then spoke:

"Hell, you ain't operated on me have you?"

"An' what if'n I have?"

"Hope you had your doctorin' hat on," Luke managed to say before he drifted off to sleep again.

Deke grinned and covered Luke's body with a blanket, he hadn't realized how cold the man was.

"Is he all right?"

Deke turned to see Jessie sitting where he'd left her but eyes wide open and bright.

"Reckon he'll be okay," he answered. "How are you feelin'?"

"Pretty good, I guess, considerin'."

"You well enough to tell me what in

tarnation's goin' on?" Deke asked.

"I think so. Trouble is, I don't know," Jessie answered.

"Well, tell me all you *do* know."

Jessie explained how she had been knocked out, down by the old ford and that when she'd come to, she was alone and she'd ridden off, but that she must've blacked out or something and . . .

"Whoa, hold it, right there. You're talking faster than a man can listen."

"Sorry, there are so many things running around my head. I unhitched the horses and rode one back to town. But again, I blacked out. I remember having double-vision, and then — nothing.

"I came to and started walking, that's when I found Luke. Luke, is he all right?"

"You dang already asked me that. Yes, he's fine. Now, where the hell is Hank?"

Suddenly, Jessie remembered the reason for her trip to town.

"Oh, God. Hank! Hank's out chasing after whoever burned our barn down again. I came to tell Luke." Jessie broke down in tears, holding her sore head in hands.

"All right, all right, calm yourself, Jessie. We'll sort this thing out." Deke said it, but even he didn't believe it.

11

IT didn't take long for the shack that had once housed Caleb Moss to burn to the ground. The only thing left standing was the cast-iron chimney and the wind would soon knock that down.

Dirk King surveyed the wind-blown embers with glee. He wasn't sure what gave him more satisfaction: screwing Bart Honer or burning down buildings, but he thought it might be the latter.

"Dirk!" Kid Weaver called out from the other side of the flames.

"Yeah, what d'you want?"

"I think you better come take a look-see yourself," Weaver replied.

Reluctantly, King tore himself away from looking at his handiwork and led his horse round to the back of the burning shack.

"Well I'll be darned," King said as

he saw what Weaver was pointing at. "That's Bart Honer's buggy. Get a load o' them fancy red-leather seats."

"I knows whose buggy it is," Weaver said. "What the hell's it doin' out here?"

King turned back to look at the pile of ash, then turned back to Weaver.

"Seems our Mr Honer may have paid a visit out here," he said.

"I'll go check," Masters said.

"Hell, no. If'n he's in there, he's a dead man. If'n he ain't in there, what's the problem?" Dirk said and lit up yet another cheroot.

"Yeah, but . . . " Masters began.

"Yeah, but, nothin'," King halted him midsentence. "Don't you see what this means?"

Weaver and Masters looked at each other and shrugged.

"Goddamn it!" King said. "I killed the sheriff, right?"

"Maybe," Weaver said.

"Okay, maybe, but he sure as hell ain't feelin' none too good, right?"

"Yeah, so?"

"An' if Honer's dead, who's over to the bank?"

Again, Weaver and Masters looked at one another. The message was getting through, and this time they didn't shrug.

"Right!" Weaver said, a grin on his face.

"We got ourselves an open town here boys. High wide an' mighty."

"I'd feel better if I jus' checked an' see if'n there's a body in there," Masters said.

"Ain't no point. Let's high-tail it out'a here, afore one of them do-gooders arrives too late to put the fires out." King was already mounting up.

"Okay," Masters said and followed suit.

The three men galloped off, heading back to Liberty and the bank.

★ ★ ★

The smoke-filled root-cellar had all but choked Bart Honer to death. He'd

162

collapsed, even though he'd covered himself in some old sacking, and been lucky when part of the wooden floor had crashed down sending flames and sparks shooting every which-way.

Although he'd escaped death for the time being, Bart Honer hadn't escaped injury. The heat had been intense, so hot that his suit trousers had, at one point, caught fire, severely burning both legs.

Honer's screams had gone unheard as the fire above raged on. In the end, he'd blacked out, his last conscious thought that he was about to burn to death.

He didn't.

Honer came to. The scream that escaped his lips was enough to put the fear of God into anyone who was within earshot. The pain in his legs was more than he could bear.

Smoke inhalation and the effort of screaming meant that his chest and throat were red-raw, and Honer, for the first time in his miserable life, truly wished he was dead.

Seated, leaning against a dirt wall, Honer tore the sacking that was covering his head and threw it to the ground. The pain coming from his legs seemed dormant at the moment, as if to lull him into a false sense of security. But, bit by bit, the pain grew.

It was pitch black in the cellar, even though half the floor had caved in, so Honer couldn't see the extent of the damage to his legs. His imagination went wild: he daren't move his legs for fear they might just drop off, yet he couldn't stay here forever.

The clouds above parted and the moon's eery light began to filter through the wispy smoke that hung around the shack as if loath to leave.

The light was bright enough in patches to see, and Honer looked down at his legs.

* * *

Hank Meadows, galloping as fast as his horse would take him was again too late to confront the badmen. The dried-out timber of Caleb's shack had, he estimated, taken less than five minutes to burn to the ground. The small barn took a mite longer, but that was due to the fresh corn that was piled inside.

Reining in, Hank jumped from the saddle. The place was deserted. Moving slowly forwards, gun in hand, Hank surveyed the dirt around both shack and barn, looking for the tell-tale prints he hoped to find.

He circled the burning embers, and found more than he'd bargained for. The horse and buggy belonging to Bart Honer was still parked out back, beside it, in the hard-packed dirt, were the impressions of the boot with the broken heel.

Not that Hank had any doubts, this confirmed that the fire-starters were the same men. He looked at the three sets of horse tracks, one set with shoes, and followed them, by the light of the moon. They headed back to Liberty.

Hank knew now where his destiny lay. For a second, he thought about going home and making sure Jessie had gone into town, but he decided against it. He could see his property from Caleb's and there was no sign of smoke or flame. Satisfied, he mounted up and was about to ride on out when a scream tore through the air that sounded barely human.

Hank froze in his saddle. Even his horse pinned his ears back flat on his head and turning his head in the direction of the now dying embers, Hank saw the whites of his eyes and the terror that filled them.

Again, the scream came. Hank looked every-which way, trying to pin-point its origin. A third scream and, impossible, Hank thought, it seemed to come from the shack!

He dismounted, grabbing his Winchester from its sheath and, cocking the lever, he tethered his frightened horse and headed back towards Caleb's place.

Silence reigned. The silence seemed deeper now after those screams, and Hank heard a ringing tone in his ears as he strained every ounce of concentration, listening for even the slightest sound.

He stood still, rifle levelled at the waist, listening. He could swear he heard tiny critters moving about in the fields, insects crawling across leaves and stalks, but nothing human.

The scream came again, a long, agonizing wail that smacked of self-pity and fear. Was it male or female? Hank wondered, he couldn't tell. It sure sounded like a woman.

There was no doubt now in Hank's mind. The screams came from the still slightly glowing embers. Gripping his rifle a mite firmer, Hank walked towards the pile of hot ash.

"Who's there?" he called out.

A wail greeted his call.

"Where are you?"

"Aaaggh! . . . Cellar!"

The shriek sent a chill through Hank even though the glow from the ashes was still hot.

Looking round, Hank found an intact shovel and, placing his rifle on the dirt in a place he could easily make a grab for if needs be, he began shovelling and scooping away the ash.

As he neared the centre of where the shack had stood, Hank halted. Most of the floorboards had gone up with the fire, but where the root-cellar was, more central and slightly to the left, there was a gaping hole that couldn't be seen from the perimeter.

"You down there?" Hank called.

"Yes, yes, yes, I'm down here," a voice replied.

So, it was a man, Hank thought.

"Hang on there, I'll try an' get you out," Hank said, but he had no idea how.

"Can you see if the steps are still there?" he called out to the man.

"Yes, yes the steps are there, only hurry, please hurry!"

"Okay, hold on there, I'm a-comin'."

Hank edged his way forwards, careful not to set himself afire as the ash below the surface was still red hot.

Peering down into the blackness, at first Hank could see nothing, but as his eyes became used to the dark, he saw a figure, lying on the dirt floor, leaning against the far wall.

"I'll jus' get a rope," Hank called down.

Carefully walking out of the ashes, Hank ran to his tethered horse and removed the lariat from the saddle and ran back.

To the rear of the shack was an old, gnarled tree that looked firm enough. He tied one end of the lariat around its trunk, held on to the coiled rope and edged back to where he thought the trap-door might have been.

"Okay, I'm comin' down!"

Testing each step before putting his weight on it, Hank descended the five rungs that led into Caleb's root-cellar. Relief flooded through him when he hit the bottom.

Striking a match, he held it high. "Mr Honer?"

"Yes, yes, it's me. I got trapped here when the shack burned down. I think my legs are badly burned. I can hardly move them."

"You hang on there, I'm gonna tie this rope round you and haul you up the steps."

"Okay, but hurry, please, I need a doctor!"

Hank looped the rope underneath Honer's armpits, then grabbed him by the shoulders and turned him away from the wall.

Honer screamed.

"Sorry, Mr Honer, but I gotta move you," Hank said.

He lifted Honer to an upright position, taking all his weight in his strong, farmer's arms.

Honer didn't scream any more, and Hank assumed he'd blacked-out, at least that would make moving him easier.

Hank managed to loop the rope round the top step and, leaving Honer hanging there like a puppet, Hank climbed the steps. He uncoiled the rope and, every muscle straining, he hauled Honer up out of what could have been his coffin.

Bending down, Hank slung the unconscious body across his shoulders and walked back to safe ground. He lowered Honer to the ground, untied the lariat from his body and the tree and recoiled it ready to hang back on his saddle.

By the light of the moon, Hank looked at the man's legs. His trousers had been burned away from the top of his thighs to his ankles, and showing through a mass of charred cloth, burned flesh.

"Jesus H.!" Hank said under his breath.

Leaving the man where he was, he got his own horse and tied it to the back of the buggy and walked the buggy over to Honer's inert body. Carefully lifting him, Hank placed him on the rear of the buggy. He had no choice now, he had to get the man into town. He only hoped Deke was around and not delivering babies or calves.

Climbing into the plush leather seat, Hank set off for Liberty.

12

DEKE WILMOT was undecided on what course of action he should take. An old man, he wouldn't be much use in a fight, fist or gun. And who else was there in town of any use? No one, that's who.

It was still too early to leave Luke, even in the capable hands of Jessie, although he was sure she'd suffered concussion — and probably still was. No, he thought, he'd have to get Sam over to keep an eye out on both Jessie and Luke.

"Jessie, I'm goin' to the saloon for Sam. I need to get out and look for Hank an' I can't leave you two alone."

"It's okay, Deke. I'll look after Luke while you're gone," Jessie said.

"Now, Jessie. You can't do that. You've got concussion, why, you could

drop off to sleep at any time. You ain't
fit enough to take care o' yourself, let
alone Luke. Now hush up and be
told."

"You're the doc," Jessie said.

"You're darn tootin' I am. Now sit
tight while I fetch Sam over."

It took Deke less than fifteen minutes
to get the services of Sam and bring
him back to the house.

"Now, Sam, I don't want you fiddlin'
with anything. Jus' keep an' eye on 'em
both. Particularly Luke. If Jessie falls
asleep, you let her lie for no more'n
an hour afore you wake her. Got it?"

"Clear as daylight, Deke," Sam
replied.

"An' *don't* touch my whiskey!"

Sam grinned.

"An' if Hank shows up, you dang-
well keep him here, I'll be back in two
hours, with or without him." With that,
Deke left the front room and walked
through to his study. There, he took
down the Winchester he kept hanging
over the fireplace and loaded it up.

From the bottom drawer of his desk, he took out his old Colt handgun and loaded it up too before strapping on the gunbelt.

It had been quite a few years since Deke had fired a gun, he just hoped it'd be a few more before he had to do so again.

He thought about taking his buggy, but decided against it on the grounds that a horse would be quicker and more manoeuvrable — albeit more uncomfortable for Deke.

Saddling up, Deke managed to get himself atop the horse, not without a certain amount of difficulty, and set off to ride the prairie in search of Hank Meadows.

He headed east and followed the trail out of Liberty towards the Meadows' place, good place as any to start, he thought.

A mile out of town and he caught sight of a crimson glow in the distance and, even this far away, he could smell smoke in the air.

Dirk King and his men reached the outer limits of Liberty to the west of the cemetery. King had enjoyed himself on the way in to town, firing up the corn fields that hadn't been harvested yet. Behind him, he had left a trail of destruction that could take years for Liberty to get over financially. But that was no concern of his.

The bank, however, was.

The fields had gone off like a Chinese cracker, the dried out stalks of corn didn't need any encouragement to spread the flames and the night wind whipped up a blazing inferno in seconds.

It was a good job neither Weaver or Masters could see the demonic expression on King's face, otherwise they would have disappeared into the night, leaving him to his own devices.

However, they hadn't, and their faith in him was still strong.

Passing through, rather than round

the cemetery, the three entered Liberty up Elm Street, heading towards Main.

Liberty felt and looked like a ghost town. There were one or two lights showing, but that was about it. The saloon showed a single light, but the double doors were closed, the livery stable doors were also closed. The general store and all the other buildings that made up Liberty were in total darkness — including the bank.

"There's an alleyway to the side and rear," King said. "I reckon we park the horses round back and smash our way in there. Okay?"

Weaver and Masters agreed. It would be foolish, they thought, even though the town seemed deserted, to try and force their way in through the Main Street entrance.

King led the way, Weaver and Masters — as ever — followed, down the dark alleyway between the bank and the saloon. The buildings, although only single storey, both had high-fronted façades that prevented most of the light from the moon from entering the alleyway, perfect for their purpose.

Leaving their horses tethered to the rear of the bank, the three men tried the rear door. Of course, it was locked. Made from wood, reinforced with a cast-iron backplate, it was impregnable.

The walls, however, were timber-clad and forcing the boards off was a simple task. Working steadily with bare hands and a single crow-bar, they made a hole in the side of the building big enough for them to enter.

Once inside, King made straight for the small floor safe.

His plan, if it could be called that, was simply to steal the safe and leave town. They could open it at their leisure.

"We ain't got no buckboard," Weaver said. "How'n the hell are we s'posed to move it?"

King hadn't even thought about it, although he wasn't about to lose face in front of them.

"There's always a buckboard parked to the rear of the livery stable, I seen it personal. Once we got the safe outside, you two can go an' get it, okay?"

"I reckon we should get it now," Masters said.

"Yeah," piped in Weaver, "this safe's gonna make a lot o' noise if'n we have to drag it across the floor. Someone might hear it."

"All right, all right! Go git it now, then." King was losing his patience, if he ever had any.

Weaver and Masters crawled through the hole in the wall and snuck round to the livery stable. It occurred to them then that the hole wasn't big enough for the safe to pass through, but they'd take care of that on their return.

King was in his element. He now had before him the means for a life of luxury. A safe full of folding money and a whole valley to choose from. He almost licked his lips in pleasure and anticipation.

At the rear of the stable, the buckboard was exactly where King said it would be, what they didn't have was harness!

Weaver tried the small rear door of the livery stable and it opened outwards. Inside it was pitch black. Letting his eyes get used to the blackness, Weaver stepped in and listened.

All he could hear was the gentle snorting of a horse to his right, apart from that, nothing.

He edged forwards, feeling his way with hands and feet as the darkness was almost impenetrable. Gingerly, he struck a match and there, not more than two feet away from him, stood Washington Cartwright.

The shock almost made Weaver fall over and he dropped the flaming match as it began to lick at his fingers.

"What de hell you want?" Washington said.

Weaver didn't answer. His pistol went off in the direction of the voice and he heard a body slump to the straw-covered floor.

"What's goin' on?" Masters whispered hoarsely from the open doorway.

Weaver struck a match and looked at the body of the fallen negro; a small red patch of blood was developing on the white shirt he was wearing.

"Nothin'," Weaver answered. "I jus' got surprised, is all."

"Hurry an' get the tackle, I'm gettin' edgy out here," Master said.

"I'm goin' as quick as I can."

★ ★ ★

Hank was driving the buggy as carefully as he could, but in the dark of the night he couldn't keep an eye out for rocks or ruts in the trail.

From behind, Hank heard the almost constant groans coming from Honer, punctuated by yells and yelps as the buggy bounced forward, getting ever closer to Liberty and Deke Wilmot, hopefully.

Riding in the opposite direction, Deke heard before he saw the buggy. He swerved off the trail, not sure who might be out driving at this time of night and rode out a ways where he could keep an eye out on the approaching buggy.

As it neared, almost level with him, he saw it was that fat bank manager's fancy wagon. He couldn't make out the driver, but Deke decided to take the chance and ride up behind it.

"Hank?" Deke called out from the rear.

Hank nearly jumped out of his skin as the voice jolted him.

He pulled hard on the reins and applied the small wood-brake, the wheels skidding as he did so.

"Deke?"

"Sure is, I jus' come out lookin' for you."

"Boy, am I glad I ran into you," Hank said. "I got Mr Honer up back, he's badly burned. I was jus' bringin' him in."

Deke dismounted and walked to the rear of the buggy. The groaning body of Bart Honer greeted him.

Deke couldn't see the total extent of the damage, but he knew it was pretty bad from the smell.

"I need to get him to my place," he said to Hank. "I already got Jessie and Luke there."

"Jessie, she all right?" Hank asked.

"She took a blow to the head, but she's doin' fine. Luke got bushwhacked someplace, he's in a pretty bad way, but, he should recover."

"Who the hell slugged Jessie?" Hank demanded.

"She never saw 'em," Deke replied.

"You sure she's gonna be all right?"

"Absolutely," Deke said. "Don't you go a-worryin'. Now, you had any joy with the firestarters yet? I smelled the smoke out yonder."

"No, I was jus' too late, but their tracks headed back in this way. They got old Arnie and Caleb's place was razed to the ground. I found Honer down in the root-cellar. I'm after 'em now."

"Best let me take the buggy in, Hank. I'll let Jessie know you're safe, you'll git to town quicker on horseback."

"Thanks, Deke. Soon as this is over, I'll come by. Tell Jessie, tell her, you know."

"Know what?" Deke said.

"Damn it to hell, tell her I love her," Hank said.

"Sure will, now you be careful, Hank."

Deke tied his mare to the buggy and clambered aboard, this being more his style of travelling anyway. Hank mounted up and, tipping his hat, rode ahead to Liberty.

"Drive carefully!" Honer yelled from the rear.

"Now don't you go a-startin' shoutin' at me, Mr Honer, else'n I might not take a look-see at you 'til mornin'. I've had a busy night already."

"Sorry, no, please, I'll be quiet, I

promise," Honer said, gritting his teeth in pain.

"Well, that's more like it," Deke said. He never did like the man anyway. Slapping the reins and yelling "G'dap", he set off at a more leisurely pace to his house.

* * *

Hank, meanwhile, had reached town. He reined in and listened. There didn't seem to be anything going on here and he began to wonder if the three riders had just ridden on.

He tethered his horse to a hitching post and, removing his Winchester, began to walk down Main Street, heading for the elbow where Elm began.

The rifle, held waist high and cocked, he moved from side to side as he scoured the street for any sign of movement.

Liberty was as silent as the grave, but three times as dangerous, he thought.

Hank swallowed, sweat was running down his face and the cold night wind made him shiver.

Scared or not, he thought, it stops here.

13

FIRES were burning now throughout the farmlands. The flames, whipped up by the night wind, were spreading far too rapidly for the handful of men and women available to combat it. It looked like a lost cause.

Cattle, those penned up and the few roaming the prairie grasslands, had long since panicked, the pens smashed down as the terror in the animals stampeded them to their freedom.

There weren't enough people available to even attempt to round them up — that would have to wait. The fire was the main enemy.

Their only hope was the fact that both Hank Meadows' place and Arnie Dillon's had been harvested, that left bare fields, only stalks visible in the rich, black earth.

The westerly wind was fanning the

flames in that direction and, with no blasting powder left and no time to ride to Liberty for more, the men hoped the empty fields would provide a fire-break. As long as the wind didn't increase, they could handle any sparks that managed to get a foothold with, they hoped, little effort.

To the west, the fire couldn't spread as quickly, the flames, jumping quite literally from corn head to corn head, were fighting a losing battle with the wind, so the firefighters concentrated on the east end of the valley.

With what livestock they could rescue, horses a few chickens and a handful of pigs, the women set off down the trail to the west and relative safety.

The smoke was hampering attempts at containing smaller outbreaks. The men, soot and dirt covered, tears filling their eyes both from smoke and the loss they were suffering, were using anything they could lay their hands on to douse the fires: sacking, shovels, and even stamping down fire with their boots.

The fire raged on. One by one, the men watched as their property was attacked: houses, barns, outbuildings and corrals added fuel to the ever-hungry flames. A lifetime's work destroyed in a matter of minutes.

Smoke became their worst enemy, the clogging white smoke choking the men, reducing visibility to the extent of their own arms at times, yet they couldn't change their positions, otherwise the fire could rage on until it hit the mountains, and then there'd be nothing left except black, burned land and ash.

With two of their number already dead, they were also anxious not to lose any more. The fine balance between man, land and animal was too crucial and the whole system could disintegrate and become untenable if reduced further.

The men fought on; they knew they'd fight 'til the last flame — or their last breath — there was no half measures. It was all or nothing.

★ ★ ★

The headache that had plagued Jessie Meadows for most of the day was beginning to recede. She no longer suffered double-vision and was starting to feel more like her old self.

Luke, on the other hand, was in the first throes of a fever, and was becoming delirious. Nothing he muttered in that half-sleep half-wake time made any sense to either Jessie or Sam.

"How long's Deke been gone?" Jessie asked.

"An hour, maybe longer," Sam replied.

They were both standing either side of Luke's body, Jessie mopping his fever-raked brow and Sam, making sure his contortions didn't land him on the floor and cause even more injury.

The bandages Deke had applied now

had a small, but still spreading circle of blood forming and Jessie was worried in case the wound had opened up completely. There was nothing she could do but wait.

"I'll put some coffee on, Jessie," Sam said. "You sure look as if you could do with some an' I know I could."

Jessie smiled at Sam, but the smile didn't hide the concern she felt for both Luke and Hank.

She continued to mop Luke's brow and he continued to utter complete drivel, then Jessie, alarmed by the sound of voices coming from the kitchen, froze, trying to hear what was being said.

She placed the cloth in a bowl of water and, making sure Luke was comfortable and not about to roll off the table, she crept, rather than walked towards the kitchen door.

The kitchen was empty. Atop the wood-burner, a coffee pot had already been set and two mugs were out on the wooden table. Her attention was caught by the fact that the back door was wide open.

Sam's Winchester was resting against the wall and without a moment's hesitation, Jessie grabbed it, cocking the lever and pushing the wooden butt firmly into her right shoulder.

She was ready for whoever entered Deke's kitchen.

The first thing she saw was Deke's back as he entered the room, followed by Sam and, between them, the moaning body of Bart Honer.

"What's going on?" Jessie asked, rifle still in position.

"Darn it, Jessie, put that rifle down will you an' I'll tell you," Deke said over his shoulder.

Jessie wasn't really aware she was still holding it. "Sorry, Deke, I heard voices and, and I guess I got a bit scared."

"Clear the table," Deke ordered, "so's we can lay out old Honer, here."

Jessie leant the rifle against the wall and took the mugs off the table. Sam and Deke gently lowered Bart Honer onto the table.

"Hold his head, Jessie," Deke said, "table ain't quite long enough. Sam, there's a plank o' wood out in the yard, bring it in."

"Sure, Deke."

Sam re-entered with the plank. "Now," Deke went on, "place the plank on the table so the end juts out and Honer here can rest his head."

As Sam placed the plank to the side of Honer's body, Deke and Jessie moved him onto it, and then all three of them pushed Honer and plank into the centre of the table.

"There," Deke said, mopping his brow, "that's better. Now let's take a good look-see at his legs."

Already, the smell of burning flesh, coupled with the coffee brewing, had filled with kitchen with a sweet, cloying aroma that had Jessie on the verge of throwing up.

"You go on back to Luke," Deke said. "I don't want him damaging himself. Sam an' I'll take care o'Honer."

"Did you find Hank?" Jessie asked, almost afraid to hear the answer.

"Oh, yeah, sure. Hank's okay. He's on the trail of whoever's behind these fires and shootin's. He's okay," Deke said and placed a gnarled hand on Jessie's shoulder. "Now, you go take care o' Luke."

Jessie, reluctantly, left the kitchen and did as she was told.

"Now, Mr Honer," Deke began, "how the hell did you get in this state?"

Before Honer could answer, Deke sent Sam to get his bag.

"Soon have you up an' about chasin' jackrabbits," Deke went on as he inspected the burned tissue of Honer's legs.

"Here's your bag, Deke," Sam said.

Without another word, Deke began removing the charred cloth that was stuck to the flesh of Honer. Piece by piece he managed to get most of it off, revealing the extent of the damage.

Where the cloth had stuck to the skin, the burning was slight, but where the cloth had burned off, there was serious burning, and Deke didn't rate Honer's chances none too high.

"Well," he said eventually, "I can clean it all up, Mr Honer, bandage it good an' tight, but that's all I can do. You'll have to trust in the Good Lord and hope no infection breaks out. Else, you'll lose your legs, maybe even your life."

Deke went to a cupboard and took down a bottle of whiskey and three glasses. "Sam, you can have one, me I'll have another, but Mr Honer, the rest is yours. You're gonna need it!"

"I didn't mean for it to go this far," Honer wailed.

"What? What you say?" Deke asked.

"I didn't plan for them to burn down everything," Honer cried out as a fresh wave of pain swept through his body.

"You sayin' you know somethin' about these here fires?" Deke said, whiskey bottle still unpoured in his hand.

Honer realized what he'd said and the terror in his eyes was replaced with fear. He nodded, silently, and closed his eyes.

"Afore I do anythin'," Deke said. "You tell me what's goin' on round here. An' you don't leave nothin' out. Un'erstand?"

Again, Honer nodded and, while Deke poured out two glasses of whiskey, one for him and one for Sam, Honer began his sorry tale.

14

WHAT light there was suddenly disappeared. Hank froze, he felt as if a giant hand had turned the wick down behind him. Looking up into the night sky he saw the reason for the blackness.

The moon, now hidden by an ominous black cloud, had disappeared, along with half the stars. It seemed as if a black-hole had suddenly appeared, swallowing everything in sight.

Hank walked on. His ears strained for the slightest sound, and the slightest sounds made the loudest noise.

A single oil-lamp burned in the saloon, throwing a thin, yellow pool of light on the boardwalk and Hank walked towards it, keeping the centre of Main.

Again he stopped. This time he heard two quite distinct sounds, the snort of a horse nearby and something heavy being dragged across a wooden floor.

Tilting his head, Hank tried to gauge the direction of the sounds but, with the wind and the dull echoes caused by the wooden buildings, it seemed to come first from the left, then the right. Then straight ahead. *The bank.*

Licking his dry lips with a drier tongue, Hank edged forwards, eyes now straining as hard as his ears watching for the slightest movement.

Passing the saloon, he peered into the blackness of the alleyway that separated saloon from bank, but with moon hidden and the shadows so thick and black he could see nothing. He swallowed, hard, and entered the alleyway.

★ ★ ★

"Come on," whispered King, "one more shove an' we'll have it right by the wall."

The three men strained a final time

and the heavy metal safe grudgingly shifted another two or three inches across the sand covered floor, gouging out parts of the floorboards.

"Dirk, how the hell're we gonna lift this thing onto the buckboard?" Weaver panted through the effort of shifting the safe.

King thought a second or two. "We'll manage," was all he said.

"Sure," Weaver said under his breath.

Reaching the wall, it was obvious to all that the hole wasn't big enough.

"Git over to the livery," King ordered, "and get something we can break the wall with some more."

Weaver and Masters looked at each other, sighed, and eventually, Master squeezed through the hole.

The cold night air hit the sweat on his face and he shivered and wiped his face with a 'kerchief. He wasn't paying much attention as he walked down the alleyway, so he didn't see Hank Meadows, his back to the saloon side wall.

A thin shaft of blue-white light pierced the alleyway. No more than three inches wide, it caught the buckle of Masters' belt and gave Hank all the warning he needed.

Slowly lowering the Winchester and leaning it against the wall, Hank braced himself. Surprise was on his side, and he knew he could take this man out, narrowing the odds from three to one to two to one.

Standing in the black-hole of shadow, Hank felt as if the man must surely see him, but he didn't. As Masters drew level, the shaft of light now aimed like an arrow at his chest, Hank drew his Colt and brought it down across the face of Masters.

For a second, Masters stood stock-still, amazement filling his dark features before the pain reached his brain and his legs buckled at the knees as he collapsed, backwards, into the dirt.

Hank was breathing heavily. He didn't realize it at the time, but from the moment he'd seen the figure emerge, he'd been holding his breath. Now, he inhaled deeply through his nose and panted through his mouth.

His hands began to shake in a nervous reaction. Was he dead?

Hank knelt down beside his stricken victim. No, he was still alive, but out cold. Hank breathed a sigh of relief. He'd never killed a man and he didn't want to start now.

Removing the man's gunbelt, Hank turned Masters over and tied his hands behind his back, then, removing his trouser belt, he tied his legs and dragged the body into the centre of Main and then re-entered the alley.

Keeping tight to the wall of the saloon once more, Hank edged his way closer to the bottom of the alley. The buckboard and two came in to view and Hank, on a whim, decided to move it.

Whispering to the frightened animals, he slowly led them up the alley and out on to Main, where he tethered them to the hitching-post outside the saloon.

Then he went into the alley for the third time, this time feeling more in control. Grabbing his rifle, Hank got to the bottom of the alley. The shaft of moonlight had disappeared and Hank even had time to gaze into the sky and watch the smaller wispy clouds scud across the moon's face. Another shaft, bigger this time, lit the bottom of the alley for a brief moment, but long enough for Hank to see the split wood littering the dirt. He saw the hole in the wall.

Inside the bank, Dirk King was edgy.

"Where the hell's he got to?" he asked Weaver, as if he should know.

"Maybe he can't find nothin'," Weaver replied.

"Then go help him look," King spat back.

Weaver looked at King and the look he saw there in the man's eyes bordered on madness.

"Yeah, right, okay, Dirk, I'll go give him a hand," Weaver said as calmly as he could. He was relieved to get out.

Squeezing through the hole, he took a long look at his old partner. King turned his back to him, lighting a cheroot and blowing a cloud of smoke into the air. He flicked the match high up and watched as it landed on the floor, still aflame.

Jesus, thought Weaver, he's gonna burn the whole dang place down!

Weaver stepped out into the alley. Hank's Colt thudded onto the back of his head and Weaver fell face down into the dirt. Again, Hank trussed him up and dragged him onto Main.

From behind, Hank heard footsteps running down the boardwalk. He dropped Weaver's legs and drew his gun as he fell to the ground.

Deke Wilmot, rifle in hand, was approaching slowly, but heavily. Hank stood, a finger to his lips, and walked across the street.

"What the hell you doin' here?" Hank whispered.

Deke nearly jumped out of his skin.

"Jesus, Hank, don't sneak up on a body like that!"

"You was making enough noise to wake the dead," Hank said.

"Listen, I jus' had a long talk with Honer. He's the one ordered your barn to be burned down."

"Honer? The bank manager?"

"The very same. Seems he was a mite greedy an' he hired a fella called Dirk King to do his dirty work, but this King was greedier still, an' took matters into his own hands."

"Dirk King, huh?"

"Yeah, an' he's got two pards with him, Kid Weaver an' Brent Masters. So I figured three onto one, you might be needin' a hand."

At that precise moment, the clouds parted and Main was hit by a bolt of blue light as the moon, free at last, shed its glow.

"Seems like you're doin' all right on your own," Deke said, staring at the two unconscious bodies lying in the street.

"You go on back, Deke," Hank said. "This is somethin' I gotta do on my own. Jus' take care o' Jessie."

"You be careful, Hank," Deke said.

"Get outta here," Hank replied and smiled.

He stood and watched as Deke walked back up Main. Then, taking a deep breath, Hank turned and headed for the alleyway once more.

Dirk King was in a silent rage. How long could it take to get a rod or something to break the wall down? He became restless and reckless.

A red tinge had appeared at the periphery of his vision as anger and frustration took a firm grip on him. He grabbed hold of the safe and, with the strength only granted to madmen, he began to push the big metal box closer and closer to the wall. Inch by inch he shifted it, sweat rolling freely, his breath coming in huge lungfuls.

The safe stuck on a floorboard and it wouldn't budge. King took his pistol out as if to shoot the safe, but thought better of it. He tried to calm himself down, but failed.

Squeezing between wall and safe, Dirk King stepped out into the alley. His rage at the two idiots he'd sent out was such that he drew his sideiron again: he was going to blow their stupid heads off as soon as . . .

"Hold it right there, mister!"

The voice brought King back to his senses. It wasn't Weaver or Masters.

Throwing himself to the ground and rolling round behind the bank, self preservation took over and King loosed a shot off in the general direction of the voice.

Hank Meadows wasn't a gunman, but he wasn't stupid, either.

As soon as he'd seen the man emerge, he'd called out and then moved on. The shot missed him by three feet, still too close for comfort, he thought, as he let loose with his rifle.

King both heard and felt the slugs rip into the tinder dry wood of the bank building, and, without showing his head, he pointed his Colt round the corner and loosed off three more shots.

Mentally, Hank counted four shots all told.

King stared frantically behind him. The alley finished in a dead end with a six-foot high plank fence. King fancied his chances of getting over it and away, back to the livery stable and the safety of his waiting horse and rifle.

He didn't like the idea of being shot at by a man he couldn't see.

Crouching now, ready to spring, King fired off another shot down the alley and leapt, headlong, at the fence.

He misjudged the distance and, although his hands were gripping the top of he fence, his body was way down low. Summoning all his might, King pulled himself up, moved an arm over the top of the fence and swung a leg over. From this position it was easy to get the rest of his body over and away.

A demonic grin spread on his face

as he landed awkwardly in the dirt on the other side. Another alley led back to Main, and he ran as fast as he could, knowing the livery stable was on the opposite side of the street.

Hank Meadows had outwitted Dirk King. Hank knew the layout of Liberty far better than King, and he knew that, once over the fence, there was nowhere else to go but Main Street. That was where Hank waited now.

He tossed his rifle to the ground; if there was going to be gunplay, then it would be a fair fight, Hank wouldn't want it any other way.

King reached the end of the alley; sweat ran down his face, leaving white lines of clean skin in its wake. King stopped, getting his breath back, and had the presence of mind to re-load his Colt. Six slugs now, more than enough, he felt.

Peering first towards Elm and then up Main Street itself, King saw the man standing slap-bang in the centre of the street. Behind him was the buckboard, and to the side of the buckboard, King made out the two bodies.

Well, looky here, he said to himself, seems the man wants to draw.

"You comin' out now, mister?" Hank said in a voice as even as he could make it.

Dirk King smiled. He'd killed nearly forty men in his time, some fair some not, but he'd yet to meet a man who could out-draw him.

"Comin' out, mister," King shouted as he emerged from the alleyway. He walked straight towards the centre of the street, almost opposite the livery stable.

For a minute, the two men stood, fifteen feet separating them. Hank was beginning to have doubts: he'd never been involved in gunplay. But, as quickly as these thoughts began to dissolve his resolve, he dismissed them. He wasn't fighting only for his life, or Jessie's; the future of Liberty and the surrounding county rested now firmly and squarely on his broad shoulders.

Dirk King was in control now. Every sinew, every muscle tensed and at the same time, relaxed. This was familiar territory to him. This was his game now.

"Make your move, mister," King said easily. He watched and saw Hank curl and uncurl the fingers of his right hand. "What're you waitin' on, mister, make your play?"

Hank felt a calmness descend on him. Suddenly, he knew he could take this man.

His right hand grabbed the butt of his Colt with a speed he didn't know he had. At the same time, his left hand came across and, with the flat palm, cocked the hammer just as he squeezed the trigger.

Quick as he was, he was a fraction slower than Dirk King. King's bullet zipped into Hank's right shoulder a split second after he'd pulled the trigger.

Hank swung round under the impact of the bullet and fell to the ground, and didn't see where his slug had gone.

Dirk King did. He stared down in disbelief at his chest; he was flat on his back watching a pool of blood spread across his shirt that seemed to be pumping from him! How could that be possible? he thought. It was his last thought. His head slumped back into the dirt, his eyes and mouth wide open, and died.

Deke Wilmot had ignored Hank's request and, instead, had hidden further down the street. At the sound of the almost simultaneous shots, he moved out onto Main, his rifle ready to shoot if Hank got hit. There was no need.

Hank was lying in the centre of Main, leaning up on his good shoulder. In front of him was a dead man.

"Never thought you had it in you, boy," Deke said.

"Neither did I, Deke, neither did I."

The sound of horses made both men turn. The long-awaited stagecoach, filled with mail and provisions and delayed with a broken axle, rumbled down Main Street. It ground to a halt outside the saloon and the driver, not taking in what was going on, shouted out to the only passenger:

"Last Stop Liberty!"

Hank looked up at Deke and grinned. "It sure is," he said. "It sure is."

THE END

TOP HAND
Wade Everett

The Broken T was big. But no ranch is big enough to let a man hide from himself.

GUN WOLVES OF LOBO BASIN
Lee Floren

The Feud was a blood debt. When Smoke Talbot found the outlaws who gunned down his folks he aimed to nail their hide to the barn door.

SHOTGUN SHARKEY
Marshall Grover

The westbound coach carrying the indomitable Larry and Stretch headed for a shooting showdown.

FIGHTING RAMROD
Charles N. Heckelmann

Most men would have cut their losses, but Frazer counted the bullets in his guns and said he'd soak the range in blood before he'd give up another inch of what was his.

LONE GUN
Eric Allen

Smoke Blackbird had been away too long. The Lequires had seized the Blackbird farm, forcing the Indians and settlers off, and no one seemed willing to fight! He had to fight alone.

THE THIRD RIDER
Barry Cord

Mel Rawlins wasn't going to let anything stand in his way. His father was murdered, his two brothers gone. Now Mel rode for vengeance.

ARIZONA DRIFTERS
W. C. Tuttle

When drifting Dutton and Lonnie Steelman decide to become partners they find that they have a common enemy in the formidable Thurston brothers.

TOMBSTONE
Matt Braun

Wells Fargo paid Luke Starbuck to outgun the silver-thieving stagecoach gang at Tombstone. Before long Luke can see the only thing bearing fruit in this eldorado will be the gallows tree.

HIGH BORDER RIDERS
Lee Floren

Buckshot McKee and Tortilla Joe cut the trail of a border tough who was running Mexican beef into Texas. They stopped the smuggler in his tracks.

BRETT RANDALL, GAMBLER
E. B. Mann

Larry Day had the choice of running away from the law or of assuming a dead man's place. No matter what he decided he was bound to end up dead.

THE GUNSHARP
William R. Cox

The Eggerleys weren't very smart. They trained their sights on Will Carney and Arizona's biggest blood bath began.

THE DEPUTY OF SAN RIANO
Lawrence A. Keating and
Al. P. Nelson

When a man fell dead from his horse, Ed Grant was spotted riding away from the scene. The deputy sheriff rode out after him and came up against everything from gunfire to dynamite.